A REFUGE IN MONTANA

ALLIE PLEITER

Recycling programs for this product may not exist in your area.

ISBN-13: 978-1-335-62165-8

A Refuge in Montana

For questions and comments about the quality of this book, please contact us at CustomerService@Harlequin.com.

Love Inspired
22 Adelaide St. West, 41st Floor
Toronto, Ontario M5H 4E3, Canada
www.LoveInspired.com

HarperCollins Publishers
Macken House, 39/40 Mayor Street Upper,
Dublin 1, D01 C9W8, Ireland
www.HarperCollins.com

Printed in Lithuania

"You want to borrow my son as a donkey rehabilitation program?"

Nick laughed out loud at that. He had one of those deep and hearty laughs. Her late husband had told her he was always looking for ways to make Nick bust out laughing for the sheer fun of it. Nick shook his head before replying, "Yeah, I suppose I do."

"You didn't plan it this way? Set all this up?"

Nick's face was a mixture of expressions. "Not this. I mean, I did hope bringing Buddy and Dunk here might mean we could begin to...talk...but I hadn't planned on the way Taylor and the donkey connect. I haven't pushed it or done anything to manufacture it, if that's what you mean."

She lowered a suspicious eyebrow. "What about the boots?"

"They were just a gift," he insisted. "An impulse. Honest."

Vicky hesitated. Not because she didn't believe Nick, but because she did. Her stalwart resistance to him and his motives was starting to fray around the edges.

Now who was being a stubborn donkey?

The bestselling author of over sixty titles, **Allie Pleiter** has sold over 1.8 million books in her twenty-year career. Allie also coaches writing productivity and speaks nationally on time management for creatives. Allie is an avid knitter, confirmed coffee junkie and firm believer that "pie makes everything better." She lives in the suburbs of Charlotte with her husband and the world's most adorable dog. Sign up for her newsletter at alliepleiter.com/contact.html.

Books by Allie Pleiter

Love Inspired

Three Sisters Rescue Farm

Rescue on the Farm
A Montana-Sized Secret
A Refuge in Montana

True North Springs

A Place to Heal
Restoring Their Family
The Nurse's Homecoming
For the Sake of Her Sons

Wander Canyon

Their Wander Canyon Wish
Winning Back Her Heart
His Christmas Wish
A Mother's Strength
Secrets of Their Past

Visit the Author Profile page at LoveInspired.com for more titles.

And be ye kind one to another, tenderhearted,
forgiving one another.
—*Ephesians* 4:32

In fond memory of my longtime agent Karen Solem

Chapter One

Of all the unpleasant, unwanted surprises in Vicky Siden's life, few topped the sight of the man standing in front of her.

As Mondays go, it had been better than most. Getting her son, Taylor, ready for preschool had gone smoothly, despite how he'd grown antsier as the summer break grew closer at the end of this week. She'd put in a few hours at her veterinarian office, but was ready to enjoy her afternoon off just being an unhurried mom of a cheerful three-year-old boy.

Vicky had spread a blanket out with lunch for her and Taylor in the pretty little park that made up High Mountain's town square. Meg Emerson and her girls would bring Taylor over when the half day from the older grades let out the same time as Taylor's morning preschool. It promised to be a lovely afternoon.

Instead, her cheerful preparations were knocked aside when she looked up from her spread to see Nick Youngston.

She'd had to blink and shake her head, startled to see the man. Nick Youngston? Here? Walking toward her?

She waited until he was standing on the edge of the blanket before she spoke. "You've got a lot of nerve." It was a good thing her son hadn't arrived. His innocent young ears should never hear the kinds of words she had for this man.

"I know." After all this time, after all that had happened, that was all he had to say?

"Do you?" she shot back. "Do you? You disappear from Roger, from us, and then just waltz in here like everything is fine?" The anger boiled up seemingly from out of nowhere, and alarmingly fast. Vicky put both hands on the blanket just to keep them from shaking. She would not give him the respect of getting up, even though the height he had over her and the shadow he threw over her picnic blanket irritated her. "You deserted Roger. You deserted Taylor and me."

Nick just stood there. "I know."

His resignation only made it worse. "You were his best friend, Nick. You were Taylor's godfather." She used the past tense like a weapon. Wanted it to hurt him. The man now standing in High Mountain had no right to be there, no right to any role in her life. Roger was gone, and it would never be anything but Nick's fault. Sure, the official report had cleared him, but to her it would never be anything but Nick's fault.

"Why are you here?"

Nick shifted his weight. "Among other things, I brought the donkey and the horse to Three Sisters Rescue Farm on Saturday."

So *he'd* been the game warden who'd brought the two animals to Three Sisters Rescue Farm over the weekend. How did Cay not realize who he was? And what did "among other things" mean?

A silence stretched between them. He didn't seem to know what to say to her, and she didn't want to say anything to him.

"I'm hoping you'll…well, I want to talk."

"I don't." Harsh, maybe, but what kind of man ambushes the widow of his best friend—*deceased* best friend—like this?

"I can understand that." He spoke with low and quiet words.

She couldn't imagine how he could claim to understand that.

"There you are!" Meg's voice came from behind Nick. "We were looking for you over by the sandbox."

The town square park was a charming spot, boasting a collection of shady trees, a swing set, and a sandbox. Taylor loved spending time here, giggling on the swings and digging in the sand. She'd had countless of these little casual park playdates with Meg and her girls.

"Mama!" Taylor called out, ducking around Nick to launch himself at Vicky in an enthusiastic hug. "I gots a star today!"

Vicky forced the irritation out of her voice to focus on her son. "Did you?"

"For asking stuff."

This was good news. Taylor was a sweet soul, cheerful with those he knew, but he often shut down in new situations. Vicky and Taylor's teacher were working on rewarding the boy for participating in class. "Good for you."

Taylor eyed her. "And you promised."

"I did," Vicky admitted. If Tyler had earned three stars in a row, they would go down the street for ice cream. "But only after you eat your lunch."

Taylor seemed disappointed that he wasn't able to convince his mother to ditch lunch in favor of immediate ice cream. "Okay." His resignation sounded like the tone Nick had used.

Her son suddenly was aware of the stranger among them. Twisting his head around and up toward Nick's tall form,

Taylor drew closer to Vicky. She watched her son fold back up into himself the way he often did with strangers. He had no reason to recognize this man, as Nick had disappeared from their life when Taylor was just months old.

"Hi there," Nick greeted. "You must be Taylor."

Taylor swung his gaze back to Vicky, as if to check if it was okay that this man knew his name.

"Taylor," Vicky said with as much civility as she could manage, "this is Mr. Youngston. He used to work with Daddy." She left out the part about being Roger's best friend. His close colleague. And his role in Roger's death.

"Hi," Taylor said cautiously. Then he leaned in toward his mother and whispered, "Is he coming to our picnic?"

Nick Youngston was most certainly not invited to today's picnic. Vicky said a silent prayer the man knew enough not to sit down.

"I'm on my way over to the farm," Nick explained, clearly having heard Taylor's whispered inquiry. "I promised Cay I'd bring some supplies over for Buddy and Dunk."

"The horsies!" Tyler's eyes lit up. He'd met them on Vicky's initial visit on Saturday and taken an instant liking to the pair. "I like 'em. Dunk has funny ears."

Nick laughed. "He does, doesn't he?"

"Did you hurt Buddy's leg?" Taylor asked, without any notion of the accusation his question raised.

Well, they had been encouraging Taylor to ask questions, hadn't they?

Cay Emerson, Vicky's aunt, and one of the three sisters who ran Three Sisters Rescue Farm, had gently explained to Taylor how someone hadn't taken good care of Buddy. That's why an infection made the horse limp. It fascinated Vicky how Taylor, often so cautious, took so quickly to the farm's newest residents.

Nick showed no offense at the question. "No, sir. I'd never do that. It's my job to take care of animals." He tried to bend down to Taylor's height, but Nick's own leg seemed to be stiff. Now that she thought about it, Nick had walked with a bit of a limp on his trip over the park grass.

"But I can tell you I made sure the bad man who let Buddy get hurt is going to be punished for it. And I think Miss Cay and your mom will do a good job of fixing him up."

"Are you going over to the farm?" Why did Taylor choose now to abandon his customary shyness? She didn't care for them to have any connection, even if Nick was Taylor's godfather. In her mind, he had forfeited that title, and she couldn't think of a single thing he could do to earn it back. There were no gold stars to be had here.

"In a bit."

Taylor turned to her. "Mom, can we go?"

"What happened to ice cream?" Vicky teased. She didn't welcome the idea of spending any more time with Nick.

"Oh, yeah." Taylor turned to Nick. "I get ice cream today for getting stars in class."

Nick's tanned face split into a smile. His wavy dark hair looked uncombed, falling over dark brown eyes and ruddy features. "So I heard. Good job, little buck."

Vicky shot Nick a dark look. *No one* got to use Roger's favorite nickname for Taylor. Even she couldn't bring herself to use it.

Nick caught the reprimand even if Taylor never noticed. He coughed and shifted his weight again. "Yeah, well, I should be going. I'll be here for a few weeks, staying at the inn over on Cedar Street, getting Buddy and Dunk settled." He looked at Vicky. "Maybe I'll see you over there a time or two."

Here for a few weeks? Why? Vicky thought about Nick's limp. Was that why he was here and not on duty with the U.S. Fish and Wildlife Service? Medical leave? She certainly wasn't going to press him for details. She tried to ignore Nick's thinly veiled request to talk. "This is the last week of school. We're busy. But thanks for bringing the animals to the farm."

"Well, okay then. I'll…just head on over to the feedstore then."

Taylor waved and started poking through the basket Vicky had set out in the middle of the blanket. "Bye! Mom, do we got apples?"

Meg watched Nick make his way back across the grass, then turned to Vicky with a dubious expression. "Was that who I think it was?"

"Yes. Let's not get into it just now." She nodded toward Taylor and the two girls now unpacking their own lunches and spreading out a blanket next to Vicky's. "I'd rather not get into it ever."

Nick walked off feeling lower than low. *That didn't go how I'd hoped. Not by a long shot.* He knew it would be hard to see Vicky again. He'd expected to see ice in her blue eyes, anger even, but she was harshly cold. Resentful.

She still blamed him.

Of course she still blamed him. And why shouldn't she? He'd spent the past three years blaming himself for Roger's death. It was why he'd disappeared after the shooting episode that took Roger's life. He didn't deserve to stay and try to be any kind of support to Taylor and Vicky.

But his efforts to run from the guilt had only made things worse, and with too much time on his hands while his knee healed, life had handed him this long shot at making things right.

Only it was going to be way harder than he thought.

It wasn't really fair to pin his hopes for redemption on a lame horse and a comical donkey, but Nick had no better plan. Three Sisters Rescue Farm was a great place for Buddy and Dunk to live out the rest of their lives. Who wouldn't want to get fussed over by the three McNally sisters: Cay Emerson, Barb White, and Peggy Davis? Those ladies had huge hearts and endless stores of optimism. If he and Vicky could spend time in that world, surrounded by all that love and redemption, wouldn't a bit of it rub off?

Nick's knee buckled as he stepped off the curb, and he caught himself with a grunt before stumbling. *You and me both, pal*, he silently called to Buddy. *We've got some healing to do.* They all did, now that he thought of it. Inside and out. Because if he'd learned anything in the long, frustrating way back from tearing his knee up in a mountainside fall, it was that sometimes you needed to heal the inside in order to heal the outside. That's really why he was here. Dunk and Buddy were just the happy accident that made it possible.

The look in Vicky's eyes stuck with him as he picked up the supplies waiting for him at the local feed store. He'd pledged to cover all the expenses for Dunk and Buddy for the first three months, unsure how they would fare in the new environment. He knew some animals couldn't come back from abuse and neglect. He knew that while "unrescuable" wasn't really a word, it was definitely a thing. The saddest of realities.

A short while later, Nick pulled his truck onto the farm property. Cay's and Peggy's broad smiles helped to settle Nick. The sisters seemed older than middle-aged but definitely young in spirit. From their reports yesterday, it seemed Dunk and Buddy had done okay their second night on the farm.

"How'd our guys do?" he asked as he got out of the truck.

"A bit skittish," Peggy replied. "Like they still weren't sure about their new home. I can't tell if they liked the dogs or found them annoying." The farm boasted eight dogs and a hutch of rabbits, with plans to add more "as God sends 'em," as the sisters like to say.

"Where do you want this?" Nick cocked his head toward the bales of straw and bags of feed in the back of his truck.

Cay shaded her eyes with her hand as she looked toward the large barn door. "Where do you think they want it?"

The sisters' naive optimism was one of the reasons Nick was staying in town for the next three weeks. Rescuing abandoned puppies and a litter of rabbits was one thing. A horse and a donkey were quite another.

"Straw underfoot, feed in their buckets." The barn had a pair of large stalls that seemed to have gone unused for years, tucked along the walls opposite the pens that housed the dogs. The rabbits were over near the door. Not a bad setup, just in need of some updating. Buddy and Dunk would stay in the same stall at first, then perhaps move to individual stalls if they seemed to want it.

Once they got enough confidence to roam around, the farm's existing field fence wouldn't do at all. It might hold Dunk, but it wasn't nearly strong enough for a horse Buddy's size. Nick planned on helping with that, too.

"You're making sure you keep in front of them?" Nick asked the sisters. Approaching a skittish horse or donkey from the rear often earned you a hard kick you didn't soon forget. That was a lesson he didn't want these nice ladies to learn.

"We are," answered Cay. "And talking to them, just like you said. They're good listeners."

Nick grabbed one of the bags of feed and walked into the barn behind Cay and Peggy. "They can be. Although I think Dunk ignores people when he wants to."

"Me, too," quipped Cay. "We'll get along just fine." She waved to the pair of animals as if they were old friends. "Hello, boys. Your friend is back."

Nick could swear Dunk and Buddy nodded their heads in greeting. There was something about those two animals, their goofy friendship and good natures intact despite all the neglect they had suffered, that called to him.

Peggy scowled. "They're so skinny. Makes me mad. It ought to be against the law to treat an animal like that."

"It is," Nick replied. "We had their owner on several other counts, but I was happy to add animal neglect to the list. He won't be back out into the mountains to cause trouble anytime soon."

"Speaking of causing trouble," Cay asked, "how'd meeting Dr. Vicky go? You seemed nervous about it."

These sisters seemed to be world-class meddlers. They clearly hadn't recognized him, a fact for which he was thankful. He had made the mistake of one tiny comment about introducing himself to Vicky on account of her being the local veterinarian, and they'd picked up on his anxiety.

Nick supposed he owed them an explanation. They'd asked him repeatedly why he'd chosen Three Sisters Rescue Farm, and he'd dodged the real answer. Now that Vicky knew he was back in town, he'd have to come clean. "Dr. Vicky and I, well, we have a bit of history."

Both sisters' eyebrows raised.

"Not the good kind."

Curiosity filled Cay's features. "Meaning?" she asked.

"I'm Nick Youngston." He'd managed to leave his last name out of the conversation so far. "I'm Taylor's godfather." That almost felt like a lie. Did he still deserve that title? "Or supposed to be. Roger was my good friend."

Peggy's jaw dropped. "You're *him*?"

If there had been any question whether Vicky had shared the story of Roger's death, there was no doubting it now. He waited for their expressions to turn judgmental. After all, Vicky was their niece, and she clearly had shared all the ways Nick had betrayed Roger, her and Taylor. Evidently Vicky hadn't shared his name, though.

"I…well… I'm looking to make things right between us. I thought Buddy and Dunk might help." Now that he was explaining it to them, this whole idea suddenly seemed far-fetched, manipulative, and scheming.

Peggy sighed. "Well, mister, you got a lot to make right the way she tells it."

Nick pressed his lips together and shrugged, wondering just how horrible a picture Vicky had painted of him. He deserved most of it, if not all of it.

Cay actually offered him a smile. She had kind, encouraging eyes. "I admire a man who isn't afraid of an uphill battle."

Uphill was putting it mildly.

"Our Dr. Vicky's a reasonable sort, but she's not afraid to speak her mind. How'd she take to you saying hello?"

Nick grimaced. "Not especially well." The ice in her response to his statement that he wanted to talk could have frozen half the county. It certainly had planted a ball of ice in his stomach. One that hadn't yet thawed despite the warm May day. One that might not thaw anytime soon. If ever.

"Early days," Peggy offered. "Just like Buddy and Dunk

here. Today's no predictor of how we'll get along eventually, right?"

Nick sure hoped that was true for people, too.

Chapter Two

Vicky had made countless visits to Three Sisters Rescue Farm. Her mother, Barb, was one of the three McNally sisters, with her aunts Cay and Peggy rounding out the trio. She considered the women not only family, but treasured friends and sources of wisdom.

It was one of Taylor's favorite places to visit, which made it easy to offer veterinary care to the animals who found their way onto the farm.

Today's visit, however, felt quite different. Partly because Vicky was not a large animal vet, and she knew horses, cows, goats, donkeys and the like had unique needs. If she were being petty about it, she could insist that the large animal vet she'd asked to come examine Buddy and Dunk handle their entire care.

That wouldn't solve the real issue, however. The true problem was Nick Youngston's presence. Much as she never wanted to see the man again, she'd have to. She probably ought to, also. It didn't take a psychology degree to know that part of the reason she seemed to be having so much trouble healing from Roger's death was the load of anger she still carried around.

Aunt Cay met her as she got out of the truck Wednesday afternoon.

"Hi, Auntie Cay!" Taylor called out from his seat in the back. Technically, Cay and Peggy were his great-aunts, but that seemed a mouthful for a three-year-old, so Cay and Peggy were Aunties while Vicky's mom, Barb, was dubbed Grannie.

"Hello there, Mr. Taylor. Come to visit our new friends again?"

"Yep!"

Vicky had tried to convince Taylor to spend the afternoon elsewhere, or even at Meg and Grant's home just next door to the farm. Anywhere but near Nick Youngston.

Taylor was having none of it. He wanted to see his "horsey friends." More annoyingly, he also seemed uncharacteristically eager to talk more with the "horsey man" because he'd brought them to the farm. How do you explain to a three-year-old what Nick had done? Was it even possible?

If she were being honest, she didn't want Taylor to like Nick even the smallest bit. Of course, that wasn't in Taylor's nature. He was quiet, yes, but he still met everyone with an open heart. It was one of Roger's better qualities, and she didn't want to squelch it in her son.

Cay pulled Vicky a small bit away from the truck and leaned in. She lowered her voice to a whisper designed to stay out of Taylor's earshot. "We figured out who Nick is. Sure you still want to do this?"

Vicky had hoped to stave off the sisters getting involved in this situation for as long as possible. They'd have no shortage of opinions, and their meddling was the stuff of High Mountain legend.

"You did?" That was fast, even by the three sisters' gossip standards. Freshly widowed with an infant, she'd left the town two counties away where Roger had been a warden in the Wildlife service and moved back to be with her family here in High Mountain. Nick had never reached out. He'd simply disappeared and she'd cut all ties. She tried hard never to mention him, even when her mood got the best of her and she lamented losing Roger the way she had. It felt easier, better to begrudge a faceless, nameless villain than to think of Nick as a human who'd lost his best friend.

Well, she'd lost her husband. And Taylor lost his father. And all because of Nick.

Roger's death was Nick's fault.

"Well," Cay continued, "he 'fessed up. Admitted he was a friend of Roger's and *somebody's* godfather." Cay cocked her head toward Taylor, who was happily making a small stuffed donkey he had pulled out of the toy box trot around the back seat. He'd begun calling the toy Dunk. "Wasn't hard to connect the dots from there."

Cay opened the back seat door of the truck cab and unbuckled Taylor. "Why don't you go in the barn and say hello to the dogs. Auntie Peggy's in there."

Taylor scrambled out of the seat and let Cay help him down out of the van. "Is the horsey man here?"

Cay caught Vicky's eye over Taylor's head. "I believe he is."

So much for avoiding that. The dark blue truck in the farmyard must belong to Nick. She'd pay more attention next time.

That set Taylor off toward the barn at record speed. "Mind what the grown-ups say!" Vicky called after him. Rescued horses weren't carousel ponies. People could get hurt. Some days it was harder than others not to be overprotective of Taylor, given the gaping loss Roger's death left in her life. And that gaping loss was a very tender spot today.

Aunt Cay touched Vicky's arm as the two of them stared after Taylor's high-speed dash through the barn's big red doors. "It's not too late. We can make do with the equine vet. Everyone would understand."

Vicky sighed. "Everyone but Taylor. Buddy and Dunk are all he talks about. He thinks Nick is right up there with Santa Claus for bringing them here." The simmer of resentment that had sprung back up last week at the third anniversary of Roger's death resurfaced just under her ribs. "What I don't understand is why he's here. Now." She yanked her bag of equipment out of the compartment in the truck bed with more force than necessary.

They started walking toward the barn, and Vicky felt that simmer rise up to a low boil. Maybe this was a bad idea. Maybe the best thing to do here was to stay away. Keep a safe distance.

"He says he wants to set things right," Aunt Cay offered.

Vicky huffed. That was an awfully noble statement from a man who'd disappeared days after Roger's death and never once checked in on her and Taylor. That's not how friendships worked, let alone the kind of deep friendship Nick claimed to have with Roger. "Too late for that." Vicky couldn't bring herself to regret the sour tone of her words.

"Fair enough," her aunt said. Cay had been widowed as well, but she'd had long, full years with her husband. Grief is grief, but Vicky still maintained the grief of a young widow—and a young widowed mother at that—was of a sharper kind. "I do wonder what God is up to here," Cay added.

"I don't think this is God up to anything," Vicky shot back. "This is Nick looking to soothe his guilt. Showing up with neglected animals in tow, hoping he can somehow make up for his own neglect to Taylor and me. It's…" She grasped for a word to describe what Nick was trying to do. "It's pointless."

"I don't think Buddy and Dunk would call it pointless. Maybe we should just muddle our way through getting them cared for, and hope for a little closure for you in the process. They're a sweet pair, those two. How they got here isn't their fault."

"They're a lot to care for. Nick is asking a lot of you all, don't you think?" *He's asking a lot of me, too. Too much.*

Aunt Cay shrugged. "Well, I suppose that's the point—he asked. We said yes, because that's what we do when it comes to farm guests." That was the sisters' term for animals that came to the farm. She never called them abandoned animals; they were farm guests. Guests who stayed forever. "We say yes unless there's a good reason to say no."

"As far as I'm concerned, I have good reason to say no to Nick's request."

Her aunt stopped walking again. "Do you?"

Nick watched Vicky walk into the barn. Her long brown hair was pulled back into a ponytail, and she wore a different color polo shirt than the one she'd had on the other day, but it also had High Mountain Veterinary printed on it. Still, he didn't need either of those clues to know she was all business for this appointment—her eyes broadcast it with cold clarity.

He took a deep breath. *Round two. You knew this wouldn't be easy.*

"Mommy!" cried Taylor, running up to his mother. "I gots to touch Dunk's nose!"

"Safely," Nick added quickly. He skipped the part about holding Taylor up to touch Dunk. Vicky might not like that.

"What did it feel like?" Vicky's face transformed when she looked at her son. It went from icy to loving in a split second. Roger had been so totally in love with her—she and Taylor were all he ever talked about. Nick had never seen a man so thrilled to be a father. It was one of the reasons Roger's death had shredded Nick the way it had. So much had been stolen along with Roger's life.

"Wet and squishy," Taylor replied happily. "It makes a squeaky noise."

Nick had noticed Dunk's wet nose and noisy breathing and wondered if it was a symptom of problems.

"Well," Vicky replied as she set down her equipment bag, "he might have a donkey cold."

Nick had to admire the child-friendly terminology Vicky used for what probably was a respiratory infection.

"They had oatmeal for breakfast, like me," Taylor went on.

A bucket of equine feed didn't really qualify as a bowl of oatmeal, but he enjoyed the smile Vicky gave the child's enthusiastic report.

"Do they like it as much as you do?"

Taylor nodded. "More."

"That's good. The first thing we need to do is get them slowly back to a healthy weight."

"Can we let 'em eat ice cream?" Taylor smirked as if this was a brilliant plan.

Nick laughed and felt the mood had lightened enough that he could say something. "I think that only works for people. But they would probably like a few carrots."

"But those are vegtublues," Taylor said, mispronouncing the word and swallowing his previous smile.

"Not to horses," Nick replied, then sent a questioning glance to Vicky. "Right?"

It was the first time she looked at him without a scowl. "Treats are good. In moderation. And I think we can err on the side of treats for now until they gain some weight."

That was as close to cooperation as he'd gotten yet with Vicky. Small win, but he'd take it.

She walked over to where Buddy stood. "I don't like his gait."

Buddy favored his left front leg. He'd noticed it felt warm to his touch and had a strong pulse that signaled an infection or abscess. "I don't like mine, either." That misstep on a steep mountainside had left Nick with a wrenched knee six weeks ago that still ached too much.

The quick glance she threw him told Nick she wasn't quite ready for any easy humor between them.

Cay, however, laughed. "You and me both. My knees can tell me a rainstorm is coming better than any weatherman." Then Cay did a very poor impression of someone who just got a great idea. "Which reminds me. I've got some really good chocolate chip cookies that just came out of the oven and I need an expert taster. Taylor, think you can help me out?"

"Sure!"

Nick and Vicky traded "who does she think she's fooling?" looks while Cay grabbed Taylor's hand. Before Nick could object or Vicky could even get a word out, Cay and Taylor headed for the big white house that served as Cay's home in the center of the property.

Nick decided it was best to let Vicky speak first. That took forever. Finally, after a long uncomfortable stretch of silence, she met his gaze.

"Why now?"

There were a hundred answers to her question, all of them a collection of regrets and cowardice. Nick walked over and began brushing Buddy's dirty coat and matted mane just to give his hands something to do.

"The short answer is I couldn't bear it anymore."

Vicky huffed, as if she didn't think whatever he had to bear even remotely compared to what she had. She was right.

"I didn't plan this," he said. "Not in the way you think."

He could almost hear the doubtful, narrow-eyed glare she must be giving him. He certainly wasn't going to look up to receive it.

Instead, he continued his explanation while he kept up the brushing. "When I wrenched my knee, a lot of things I thought were sure bets were up in the air. Whether I would heal enough to go back to the field or end up in a desk job. The dumb things I'd done wrong when I slipped and fell." He stopped the brushing for a moment before adding, "Which got me thinking of all the things I did wrong on that *other* day." There was no need to clarify which other day he was talking about. Nick's life had divided itself into two halves—the time before Roger was killed and the time after. It must be like that for Vicky, too, only a thousand times worse.

He paused in his explanation, giving her space to say something if she needed to.

She remained silent.

So he went on. "When I came across these two, the idea of bringing them here just sort of jumped into my head. And wouldn't leave. I knew I couldn't come waltzing into High Mountain and ask to make things right for you and Taylor. I haven't earned that, and I know it. But these two, well…maybe I thought it would give us somewhere to start. A reason to talk." He looked up from the brushing. "We have a lot to talk about."

The ice hadn't quite left her eyes. "I'm not so sure that's true."

Buddy shifted his weight and brought his body closer to

Nick's. The horse version of a hug, he supposed. After all, people hadn't done right by Buddy by a long shot, yet the horse still seemed ready to give humanity another chance.

Nick walked out from next to Buddy to stand face-to-face with Vicky. "I'm sorry," he began, working hard to push the words out from a dark place in his chest. "For what happened to Roger, for what I didn't do to stop it, and for how I behaved afterward. I know it doesn't change anything, but I am sorry."

A part of Nick hoped the weight that had been pushing down on him for years would lift slightly when he apologized to her in person. And owned up to the colossal regret and shame that had hounded him since that fateful day on the mountain.

The truth was that it changed nothing. It just was hanging in the air between them. After all, what kind of reply could she give to such a statement? It's okay? I accept your apology? Neither of those applied.

"You should be sorry." Vicky's words had a sharp edge that told him she'd waited a long time for his apology. He didn't doubt that. Still, Nick was surprised that it seemed more a statement of fact than an accusation.

"Yes, I should," he admitted. Nick half expected her to turn on her heels and walk out of the barn. When she didn't, he continued. He'd rehearsed this speech a dozen times, and still the words came out in fumbling bits. "And I…it seems to me that real apologies…well…they're only true if things change. If you take action on account of them. If you change what you're sorry about. I want to make that happen here, if you'll let me."

Vicky shifted her weight, looking everywhere around the barn except at him. She wrapped her hands around her waist. "You can't change that Roger is gone."

There was so much pain in those words. "No." Could she see how much that burned inside him? The thing he could never fix, never take back, never restore? Would she ever see past her own deep pain to recognize his? Did he have a right to expect her to?

Nick pressed on, determined to say what he'd come a hundred miles to say. "But I'm hoping to fix the other things. To make good on the promise I made to your husband. To Taylor's father. The promise I've failed—totally failed—until now. All I'm asking is that you let me try."

Vicky fought back the tears he could see welling up in her eyes. "I don't know that I can."

"The first time I tried to get Buddy and Dunk into the trailer to come here, they wouldn't budge." Nick wasn't quite sure why the story came to him now, except that it applied, sort of. "They didn't trust me. Had no reason to. Why would I—this new human showing up out of nowhere—be different than the cruel men they'd known before?"

Vicky shifted her eyes toward the horse and donkey, as if they'd confirm Nick's story. Buddy and Dunk, of course, made no comment.

"I had to stay there. I spent the night there, just talking to them for hours." He gave a small laugh, remembering all the sad and sorry details he'd poured out to the two animals. "They're incredibly good listeners, these two. By morning, they let me lead them into the trailer."

Vicky turned back to look at him. Nick hoped the slight softening he saw in her eyes was the beginning of understanding.

"That's all I'm asking for. Some time. If at the end of it you want to have nothing to do with me, I'll walk away. Just…not…yet."

Nick waited. He'd wait for as long as it took.

It did take a while, but eventually Vicky sighed and said, “Maybe.”

One word sent the world turning in the right direction again.

Or so he hoped.

Chapter Three

"Oh, my," Meg said with a frown the moment Vicky walked into the Sundial Diner the next morning. "Do I even need to ask who rained on your parade today?"

As if this week wasn't hard enough, today was already proving to be one of those days, and it wasn't even ten o'clock in the morning.

"No, you don't," Vicky replied. "Well, not really."

It wasn't exactly Nick Youngston that bothered her this morning. It was Taylor's ease with the man yesterday. Taylor had no idea Nick was his godfather. He'd been weeks old when Roger was killed, and out of sheer spite for his unforgivable disappearance, Vicky had never spoken of him to her son.

No, to Taylor, Nick was just "the horsey man" who had brought Buddy and Dunk to the farm.

Vicky slipped onto the counter stool in front of Meg, grateful for the steaming mug of coffee the diner owner immediately set in front of her. Breakfast at the Sundial was a High Mountain tradition, with all the regulars gathering there several times a week to share news, good food, and the not-so-occasional heaping portion of town gossip.

"So it's not Nick Youngston?" Aunt Cay asked from one stool over, where she was enjoying her own breakfast.

"No. Not really," Vicky replied. "It's something Taylor said." In her mind she again heard the simple question Taylor had asked over breakfast. Five words that had been on a loop in her head ever since.

Meg set the coffeepot back in place and leaned her elbows on the counter. "What'd he say?"

Vicky looked down into the darkness of the brew. For a moment she wasn't sure she could actually recount the stinging words. "He said 'What color was Daddy's eyes?'"

A widow herself, Meg immediately understood the weight of the question. "Oh, hon."

Vicky felt the tightness she'd been fighting all morning return to her throat. "He'd said it as he colored in a face on a coloring page." She swallowed hard. "He'd had to ask."

"How do they know just how to break our hearts like that?" Meg commiserated.

"I try so hard to make sure Taylor has some kind of memory of Roger. We have photos all over the house. But he didn't know." Vicky fought back the surge of guilt and regret that hung over her like a rain cloud.

Aunt Cay touched Vicky's arm. "He was an infant when Roger died. And while that's so very, very sad, it's not your fault."

"Yeah," she nearly muttered. Some part of her knew that. It wasn't Taylor's fault. It wasn't really her fault either—although a fierce pang of guilt sliced through her all the same. It wasn't Roger's fault, although sometimes she couldn't quite tamp down all the irrational anger for him being gone. "And here comes Nick Youngston, asking me to make it not his fault."

"And maybe that's the real point right there," her aunt said. When Vicky glared at her, Cay went on. "You just said how important it is that Taylor has as many memories of Roger as possible. Now one of the few people who knew him as well as you did has come back into your life. Back into Taylor's life."

"I'm not sure he has that right," Vicky nearly muttered.

"This kind of thing is almost never about having rights. Mercy doesn't work that way. I didn't realize who Nick was when he brought Buddy and Dunk here, but Peggy, your mom, and I all felt the strong conviction to say yes, even though we knew it would be a big job. I'm starting to think our yes wasn't just for Buddy and Dunk."

Resistance stiffened Vicky's back. "So I should make peace with Nick? After everything that's happened?"

"Sometimes forgiveness is one of the hardest things God ever asks of us. Don't you want Taylor to see you living up to that challenge?"

Was she ready to lay down the sword of blame she'd been carrying since Roger's death? It felt safer to keep blaming him as well as the poacher who'd shot Roger. Some part of her acknowledged that if there was anyone to blame for the fact that Taylor didn't know which color crayon to pick up and color those eyes on his paper, it was that poacher on that mountain. That was the man who cut Roger's life short. The man who'd fired that rifle.

Even so, blaming him hadn't brought Vicky much peace. She'd be fine for weeks, and then something like this morning would happen and all the pain would surge back up. Grief was cruel that way, always knocking you over when you least expected it. Maybe she needed one less person to blame in the world, even though it felt impossible for that person to be Nick.

"How did you answer Taylor?" Meg asked.

Vicky pulled in a deep breath, much as she'd done before answering Taylor. "I told him he had his father's blue eyes, bluer than mine, and that it was one of the things I loved best about him."

Aunt Cay immediately pulled Vicky into a hug. "Well, if that isn't the best answer ever, I don't know what it is."

It had made Taylor grin and pick up the blue crayon as if it were nothing. Not a moment of unexpected heartache.

"Thanks, Aunt Cay."

"Parenting is hard," Cay agreed. "I feel like a mother to all these animals, and they puzzle me most days. But it feels good when you get the hard stuff right, and you did that today. You take the win on this one, you hear?"

Her aunt's heart was as big as the land around her. Vicky often wondered if the animals that came onto the farm had any inkling of how fortunate they were. She liked to believe they did. Animals recognized so much more than most people gave them credit for.

"How did you answer Nick?" Meg inquired. "You said he's asking to come back into your and Taylor's life."

"My initial impulse was a hard no. Go away and don't come back."

Meg caught Vicky's wording. "And your answer now?" She set an English muffin with raspberry jam in front of Vicky. Meg knew everyone's breakfast orders by heart, as well as how folks took their coffee.

"I managed a *maybe*."

Aunt Cay smiled. "*Maybe* is a good answer. *Maybe* gives God lots of wiggle room."

Sometimes Cay Emerson's theology stumped Vicky. On the one hand, Aunt Cay seemed open to anything—and any animal—God sent her way. This meant Vicky often got a front-row veterinary seat to the three sisters biting off more than they could chew. Still, Three Sisters Rescue

Farm always managed to eke out a happily ever after for every animal on the farm. The same was likely true for Buddy and Dunk, even if Vicky wasn't thrilled about who had brought them there.

"Nick's been working with Buddy and Dunk every day," Aunt Cay went on. "Did you know he grew up on a horse farm? He has horse training skills. It's amazing to watch." After a moment, she added, "Although I think his own wounds are part of what makes him so good at it. The man is a bit of a lost soul in his own right."

Vicky wasn't eager to feel pity for Nick Youngston. Especially because he'd disappeared when things got tough. She'd never had that option.

"He was doing this thing yesterday where he walked Buddy around in a circle over and over, talking to him. Then he began walking him around the farm, past the different animals and Meg's daughters and such."

"The girls loved it," Meg said. "They said it was like a parade."

Vicky tried not to let it bother her that everyone seemed to think Nick Youngston was so nice.

"That got me thinking," Aunt Cay continued. "We've been trying to decide what to do for a farm fundraiser this year. I think we should do a pet parade."

"A pet parade?" Vicky asked, wondering if this was another episode of the three sisters' oversized optimism.

"People could parade their pets all around the square. And those that don't have pets can parade the ones from the rescue farm." Cay grinned at Vicky. "Couldn't you just picture Taylor smiling and waving sitting on top of Dunk as they trot around the square?"

Vicky could picture it. Too easily. And that was the most unsettling thing of all.

* * *

Nick tried to rein in his irritation as he walked into High Mountain Veterinary the following afternoon.

"Is Dr. Vicky available?" He hoped he kept his tone civil.

The cheerful woman behind the counter raised one eyebrow. "Do you have an animal emergency?"

Probably not that many people walked into this office demanding to see the vet without some kind of animal in tow. In truth, the only crisis at that moment was his temper. "Sort of a personal matter," he grunted.

She raised an eyebrow at that, but rose from her seat. "Let me go check. Who should I tell her is asking?"

"Nick."

"Nick…" She prompted him for a last name.

"Just Nick'll do." After all, it seemed if everyone in High Mountain didn't know who he was already, they soon would. Especially after the visit he'd just had to the town supply store.

The young woman ducked down the hall while Nick paced the waiting room, grateful no one was sitting there. He took a few deep breaths and tried to work out just what he wanted to say, but his dark mood was running off with his good sense.

He was just finishing his fifth lap of the room when the young woman came back with a questioning look on her face. She pointed down the hall. "Room 3."

Nick pushed open the door to Room 3 to find Vicky standing there with her arms crossed, looking as if he'd just invaded her space.

He wasn't feeling much friendlier. "Just how many people know?"

"Know what?" she asked.

"I suppose I could say that I'm Taylor's godfather and

Roger's friend, but I think the real question is how many people know just what you think of me."

"People saw you standing next to me at Taylor's baptism."

The reminder of those promises—and how badly he'd broken them—just made things worse. "That was two counties away and three years ago. So how does Wally at the supply store know? I went there to see about better fencing for the farm, but what I got was a lecture on the role of godfathers."

Vicky did not reply.

"I didn't realize I was public enemy number one in High Mountain."

"You aren't." She didn't sound very convincing.

"Should I be afraid to go to the grocery store now? Avoid having lunch at the diner?" He'd actually considered going to the church this coming Sunday, but after the past hour, it seemed like an unpleasant prospect to say the least.

"Well, having any meal at the Sundial is usually a front row seat to town gossip," she offered. "I guess I owe you an apology."

That surprised him.

"I may have…spouted off…to Meg the other morning when I was upset. She's a friend, and she owns the place. I was sitting at the front counter with Aunt Cay, and I guess I forgot we weren't the only ones in the diner."

He hadn't expected a warm welcome, but he also hadn't expected her to be tearing him down in public. The thought that he likely deserved it sank home more than before. What he'd done had truly, deeply, maybe irrevocably wounded her.

"Okay, but Wally?"

"I guess he didn't mention it."

"Mention what? That he happened to be sitting in the diner when you listed my sins? No. He said a lot of other stuff—a *lot* of other stuff—but not that."

Vicky's shoulders lost their battle-ready tension. "Wally is *my* godfather."

That sucked some of the air out of Nick's annoyance. "The man has some strong opinions about what that means."

She almost laughed. "I'm sure he does. But he's a good man. Does a lot for the farm and the whole community. He shouldn't have laid into you like that."

The constant, condemning voice in the back of Nick's head said *maybe he should.* "I'll get over it," he replied instead. "I'm gonna have to."

"Have to?"

"Well, I was in there talking to him about how the fencing at the farm right now is okay for dogs and bunnies and such, but not for horses. And whatever else is going to end up on that farm. They need stronger fencing."

"True." She leaned against the exam table that sat in the room beside her. He'd surprised her with that assessment. Maybe not for practical reasons—she likely knew the farm's current fencing was inadequate—but maybe because he was making it his business.

"I expect I don't have to tell you fencing is expensive and a lot of work."

"Also true," she agreed.

"So Wally cut me a deal. If Cay and her friends can raise half the cost of the fencing, Wally and I will put in the labor to install it. He seems to think it's a worthwhile penance for me."

Nick had been irked at the idea at first, but it only took a few moments for the idea to make sense. Building the fence kept him in High Mountain for a while. It gave him a reason other than his own guilt to stay connected to the farm and hopefully to Vicky and Taylor. It was good for Buddy and Dunk. And it gave him a way to be useful.

Vicky got a strange look on her face.

"What?" he questioned. Did she find the idea of his help so distasteful?

"Aunt Cay would call this one of her 'God showing up' moments."

Nick scratched his chin. "Huh?"

"She got the idea yesterday to host a pet parade as a fundraiser for the farm. It was one of the other things we talked about at the diner." She bit her lip. "It wasn't one hundred percent complaining."

"Just my failures and a pet parade?" Nick couldn't decide if that meant he should try eating at the diner or avoid it at all costs.

Vicky looked down and ran her finger along the edge of the exam table. "It was something Taylor said. I was extra upset."

It was the most personal thing she'd said to him yet. Her wounded tone made him want to know. "What'd he say?"

Vicky paused for a moment, and he wasn't sure she was going to actually tell him. "He asked what color Roger's eyes were." Her voice broke the tiniest bit when she added, "I've told him dozens of times but he couldn't remember."

Roger had gone on and on about how his baby son had his eyes. And a son that had no memory of his father or his eyes. How many thousands of other memories had Roger's death stolen? How much endless pain could Nick have prevented if he'd just been man enough to break the rules? To go back Roger up on a risky encounter with poachers instead waiting to follow official procedure?

"Taylor has Roger's eyes," he declared, even though he

knew Vicky knew that. "Taylor has a godfather. Roger still has a friend. And that fence is going to get built. I promise you that. And if there is one thing I will not do right now, it's break another promise."

Vicky held his gaze for a long, raw moment. Nick felt this was a tipping point, a sign whether he'd get anywhere in his quest for redemption. One of Cay's "God showing up" moments, indeed.

"Okay," Vicky said. Then she nodded curtly and headed out of the room, leaving Nick to stand there alone, shaking his head.

God sure had a funny way of showing up in this town.

Chapter Four

While donkeys were stubborn, today a horse was winning the prize for Most Uncooperative.

"Come on, Buddy," Nick pleaded in a low voice Saturday morning. He was standing on the far side of the barn enclosure where Buddy had been pacing for the past half an hour. "Let's not backslide."

Nick wasn't even facing Buddy. He was standing still a good distance away from the animal, listening to all the sounds of Buddy's anxiety. Pacing, snorting, short exhales all signaled that Buddy was struggling to settle down.

Cay had called him this morning with her concerns. Buddy hadn't eaten. He seemed skittish. He kept walking along the edge of the barn enclosure.

She wasn't wrong to call. It had only been a week since Buddy's arrival on the farm. Buddy was still so underweight that his ribs clearly showed under the horse's irritated skin. The horse needed a lot of good meals, a lot of good brushing, and a stronger sense of security.

"I can't do much for you if you don't let me close," Nick told the empty air in front of him, willing Buddy to hear. He'd made so much progress with the two animals in the past week that this sudden relapse bothered him immensely.

As if he'd understood him, Dunk came around in front

of Nick. Not right up to him, but far closer than Buddy. Nick turned just enough to be able to look at the comical donkey. “That’s how it’s done,” he said. “Close makes all kinds of good stuff possible.”

Dunk was also thin—maybe even more so, given his smaller size—but at least the donkey had managed to eat all his feed and nibble on hay. And Dunk wasn’t given to the constant, worrisome pacing that Buddy was prone to. “Want to go convince your friend here that things are okay?”

Dunk just batted his enormous brown eyes at Nick and cocked his head to one side like a giant puppy. Ears pinned back—in either horse or donkey—signaled fear, anger, or annoyance. Ears pricked up and forward like Dunk’s currently were meant that Dunk found Nick interesting. Worth investigating. That wasn’t totally trusting—that would take no small amount of time—but curiosity was a vast improvement over fear.

“Steady. Everything’s good here.” Nick spoke in slow, soft tones. He did not move toward Dunk, but stayed still until Dunk took a few small steps in his direction. “That’s it. We’re friends. Everything’s good.”

He listened for Buddy’s reaction to Dunk’s approach. Nick didn’t need to look behind him to know that Buddy was watching Dunk. Watching to see what Dunk did, and what Nick did in response.

Growing up around horses had taught Nick a lot about himself and about life. He’d always been a man short on patience, hungry for control. And it wasn’t just the horses who’d “rewired him” as he liked to put it. Having his knee shredded into an unusable tangle had done a number on him, too. He’d never want to go through another injury like that, but Nick recognized that it had changed him. Shaped him into a man better suited to deal with these animals.

But had it also shaped him into someone better suited to deal with these people? That remained to be seen. Especially the two people who mattered most.

A blunt bump on his elbow knocked him from his thoughts. He hadn't noticed Dunk's proximity. But there, pushing his soft black nose against his arm, was Dunk.

Victory.

For it had become obvious to everyone in the short time these two were on Three Sisters Rescue Farm that where Dunk went, Buddy often followed.

Could it work for people? Like, where Taylor went, could Vicky follow? If there was ever a question that required patience and a surrender of control, that was surely it.

"Hey there, Dunk," he greeted softly. "How's it going?"

Dunk's ears twitched and he shifted his weight from one front hoof to another. He licked and chewed—another sign of relief. He was going to be adorable when he got healthy. Right now he was cute, but in a sad, pitiful way. So much so that it was a major challenge to keep Cay from wanting to hug the guy.

"I just want to throw my arms around his neck and give him a bath!" Cay had exclaimed on more than one occasion. Nick had firmly explained to her that those actions were more likely to end with a swift kick and a nasty bite than any kind of affection.

"You're going to have to wait out his stubborn nature," Nick had said.

Cay's response was to declare, "You've never met my son, Grant. He's more stubborn than Buddy and Dunk combined."

"I give you good odds here, boy," Nick said. "You're gonna have a great life from here on in. Way better than what you knew, I guarantee it."

* * *

Some Sundays, coming to church with Taylor was a true joy. Vicky worked hard to give her son the foundations of a deep faith. She yearned for him to know that, despite the dark start they'd had in life, God's world was still a wonderful place.

Today was not one of those days.

Sometimes there were days when Taylor was as stubborn and contrary as, well, as Dunk. He didn't want to wear shoes. His shirt was too scratchy. He turned his nose up at what she'd set out for breakfast. The list was so long that Vicky found herself shamefully grateful to leave him at children's church and settle into the first quiet moment of the morning in a back pew.

Keep me grateful, Lord. Some days this is just so hard.

She knew, on some level, that Nick's appearance in her life had brought up a whole host of rough emotions. His declared intent to set things right only threw a glaring light on everything she hadn't really worked through. Old anger. Frustrations that seemed to have no solutions. Resurgent sorrows.

She found it no coincidence that today's sermon focused on redemption. To be honest, she'd never much liked the parable of the prodigal son. Her sense of fairness always sided too easily with the loyal, slighted son. Part of her knew it was God's grace and the right thing to welcome back the wayward son who'd squandered all his father's riches. Another part of her heart dug its heels in against the grace the way she'd seen Dunk dig his heels into the straw when he didn't want to be moved. Charming as the donkey was, it wasn't a complimentary comparison. *You have so much work to do in me, Lord. On the outside, everyone tells me I'm doing so well. Surely You see the mess I still am.*

At the end of the service, Vicky made small talk with people the way she always did. Sundays at Grace Community Church were also a weekly mini family reunion with all three aunts and a collection of cousins. She took joy in the happiness of her cousin Grant and her friend Meg. Grant had once been a grump of the highest order, but Meg's love for him had changed that. It gladdened her to watch her cousin turn into a first-rate father to Meg's girls, Tabitha and Sadie. The girls had lost their father and God had sent a new one in Grant. Shame pinched Vicky's chest at the shard of envy she felt. She knew better than to believe the whispers in her heart about how the same might never happen for her and Taylor.

She buried the uncomfortable emotions in a big wide grin for the newest member of the family, baby Anson. "Look at you, big boy!" Anson had endured a special surgery even before he was born to address a spinal defect. His movements were slightly wobbly, and his parents, Vicky's cousin Carly and her husband, Jack, had a long uncertain road ahead of them. Still, they adored their son and filled his life with love and possibility.

How would she address the emotional challenges that lay ahead for Taylor? Life without a father. Life with a mother still struggling with grief she worked so hard to hide.

Focus on the good all around you. Vicky grasped Anson's hand and gave it a kiss. "So good to see you. I think you've grown an inch." She told her weary heart to soak in all this young family's optimism and gratitude. *Be glad. Be grateful. Be the resilient mother Taylor needs.*

A few moments of cooing over the baby made her feel a bit brighter. But that dissolved when she looked up to see Nick. He stood in the back of the church. His presence surprised her, but not his expression. Nick wore the same cautious, doubtful expression the man seemed to continually wear. As if he hadn't quite been given permission to take up space anywhere, much less in the back pew of Grace Community Church.

He'd been watching her, looking down when she caught sight of him, but then looking back up again.

He was clearly waiting for her. The realization tightened her stomach. Nick always seemed to be looking for more than she was ready to give, and she didn't like that. It made her feel petty and ungenerous and just plain tired, to be honest. Nick was a layer of complexity she didn't want in her life right now.

Still, Meg and Aunt Cay—and even her own mother—were right: she had to get over her resistance. She had to lay down the grudge she'd been nursing against this man. He had things to give Taylor, things Roger was no longer here to give. Hard as it might be, she owed it to herself, and to Taylor, to find a way to grant the forgiveness Nick was seeking. She just didn't know how to get there in her heart.

Maybe it starts by getting there with your feet.

Vicky willed her feet to walk down the church aisle to where Nick stood, hands stuffed in his pockets. He'd dressed for church, swapping out his usual jeans, boots, and workshirt for a button-down shirt, khaki pants, and a shiny pair of cowboy boots. She could almost laugh at how his hair seemed to refuse to stay combed, a cowlick over his forehead sending locks in scattered directions. Roger had always joked about how Nick was the looker of the two, how he'd always considered it God's special blessing that Vicky fell hard for him rather than someone as ruggedly handsome as Nick.

But Nick didn't have Roger's eyes. Or his heart. Or, as far as she was concerned, Roger's deep sense of duty. And he wasn't Taylor's father. A stubborn piece of her heart still held tight to the belief that Nick was the reason Taylor had no father. The reason she sat without a husband beside her in the church pew.

All that made it doubly hard to keep her feet walking toward Nick.

"Good morning," she forced out. Maybe the only way through this was to *be* nice to Nick until she *felt* nice toward Nick. For Taylor's sake, if nothing else.

Nick nodded. "Morning."

He raised his hand as if to tip his hat in greeting, then seemed to remember he'd not worn a hat into church. That half explained his fish-out-of-water appearance—Nick was not a churchgoing man. That meant he'd come to see her, or to show himself in church to her. Neither one felt like a comfortable prospect.

She attempted polite conversation. "Did you like the service?"

"I suppose."

That made Vicky laugh. "I suppose" was the answer Roger gave when he didn't want to commit to a no or an "I'd rather not." Had Roger learned that little conversational dodge from Nick?

"Why'd you come?" Shc ought to have been ashamed of such a sharp question, but it came out of her anyway.

"I had something for Taylor, and I figured I'd find you both here." He looked around. "Where is the little guy?"

Even though he complied with her request not to call Taylor Little Buck, it bothered Vicky that he used such an amiable term for her son. So many things about Nick got under her skin. "The kids have their own Sunday School church and classes. I'm headed over to that part of the church to pick him up now."

"Can I come with you?"

"How about we meet you outside?" she offered instead.

He shrugged. "Sure." With that, he turned and walked out the church door toward the parking lot.

Her mother shot her a look—a silent "everything okay?"—from a few pews away. Vicky nodded, despite the unsettled feeling currently rolling around her insides. She owed Nick nothing. She had the right to be careful, setting limits on Nick's access to Taylor.

Of course, Taylor didn't see it that way at all. "Horsey man!" he called out as Vicky led him across the parking lot to where Nick stood by the dusty dark blue vehicle she now recognized as his truck.

"Hi there, Taylor." With a wince, Nick hunched down to Taylor's height—no small feat, since he was a large man—and held up a palm. Taylor's pint-size high five made Nick smile. It was a tight smile, the kind rusty from lack of use. The kind Grant used to have, now that she thought of it. Tabitha and Sadie once said Grant's smile was broken. All too often, she felt the same way about her own. Was Nick's as well?

"I was over at the farm supply store yesterday, and I saw something I thought you might like. If it's okay with your mom, that is." He sent a questioning look toward Vicky before rising with another wince and reaching into the back of the truck.

Vicky wished she'd asked Nick what it was he brought before meeting him out here. She shot up a silent prayer that nothing objectionable was hiding in that truck bed before replying, "We'll see."

Nick pulled up a tiny pair of knee-high rubber muck boots. They looked to be just the right size for Taylor. He'd grown out of his current pair, recently complaining that they squished his toes. If he was going to be spending time in the Three Sisters Farm barn, he needed a new pair.

From anyone else, she'd be tickled that the gift had come at the perfect time. But these were from Nick, and that threw up a brick wall to her gratitude.

"Barn boots!" Taylor squealed with delight. "New barn boots!"

"You like 'em?" Nick asked, setting them on the ground in front of Taylor. "Wally said they were the right size. And they've got strong toes so yours will be safe around Dunk's and Buddy's hooves."

"Mommy, look!" Taylor picked up one of the boots and admired them with glee. "Blue boots!"

Did Nick know blue was Taylor's favorite color? It could have been an easy guess, or there could have been only one color choice.

Taylor picked up the other boot, holding the pair up to Nick with a wide grin. "Blue's my favorite color."

"No kidding?" Nick said. "Mine, too."

Again, a Dunk-worthy irritation scratched at Vicky's insides.

"Is it okay?" Nick asked her.

Of course, that was a nearly pointless question. No mother would ask her delighted son to give back a perfectly good pair of blue muck boots just because she had issues with the gift giver.

"Yes, it's fine." Vicky wasn't sure she'd completely hidden her hesitation.

Something in Nick's eyes told her he'd caught on. "Didn't mean anything by it, they were just there and I wanted to do something nice."

"It is nice," she made herself say. It was. "What do you say, Taylor?"

Taylor, who was busy hugging the boots to his chest like a grand prize, looked up at Nick and gushed out a loud "Thanks!"

Then, after only a moment's hesitation, he asked, "Can I put 'em on?"

After the battle she'd had getting her son to wear his sneakers this morning, Taylor's instant acceptance of this new footwear irritated Vicky more than she would have liked. "Of course."

Nick immediately walked over and opened the tailgate of his truck. "Hop on up out of the dirt."

It was the most practical place for Taylor to try on the boots, but Vicky still stiffened at how easily Nick lifted Taylor into the truck bed. It felt irrationally wrong to see Taylor in Nick's arms. Vicky found herself hugging her arms to her chest to keep from snatching her son back from the perfectly innocent encounter.

Taylor kicked his sneakers off so fast she ended up practically lunging to catch them as they sailed off the truck. Thankfully, Nick didn't try and help Taylor—she wasn't ready to see that. Instead, he held back, letting Taylor fumble with the high rubber boots until he got them on all by himself. When he did, Taylor stood up to plant his feet in a wide superhero stance.

Vicky couldn't help but smile and let a small laugh escape her. Nick stepped farther back, gesturing to her to help her son down off the truck bed.

Taylor instantly clomped around the parking lot, enjoying the feel of his new boots. "Can I go show Bobby?"

One of Taylor's best friends from preschool was just a few feet away, and many of the cars had cleared out of the church parking lot.

"Sure," she replied. The words came easier, without the tight caution she'd been fighting before.

"You sure it's okay?" Nick asked. "I know I should have asked first. Honest, it was just an impulse." He seemed genuinely contrite. It looked odd—charming almost—on his big, gruff features.

"You should have asked first," she conceded. "But in this case I think it's okay. He did actually need new boots." She surprised herself with another small laugh. "The trouble might be getting them off him. I might have to pry them off in his sleep."

Nick laughed. She'd not remembered what a big, hearty laugh Nick had. Laughter—well, the grown-up version—was such a rare thing in her life since Roger passed.

"I'm glad he likes them. He'll need them, that's for sure. And I want you to know I plan to be extra careful with Taylor's safety around Buddy and Dunk. I don't have to tell you animals with that kind of history can be unpredictable, even when they start to settle in."

"That's absolutely true." As a vet, Vicky knew that perhaps even better than many of the ranchers and farmers in the area. She was always urging her mom and aunts to be cautious. "I appreciate you being careful where Taylor's concerned. Where anybody's concerned, for that matter."

"Hard-toed boots," Nick said, as they both turned to watch Taylor taking pint-sized giant steps around the parking lot. "Good start, huh?"

She didn't want to agree with him. She didn't want to give him the benefit of having done something nice for Taylor.

But he had. And she owed him that much.

"Good start."

Chapter Five

Wally rang up the last of Nick's purchases and loaded them onto the cart. "How'd the boots go over?"

It was the friendliest question Nick had gotten from the man. Wally's demeanor toward Nick last week had been closer to a reprimand than any friendly inquiry. This week, Wally actually looked as if he wanted to know. Given that Wally had been the one to suggest the boots, Nick supposed he had skin in this game—which was odd, but welcome.

Nick shrugged. "Depends on who you ask."

Wally managed a chuckle at that. "So, if I ask Vicky, I'll get one answer, but if I ask Taylor, I'll get another?"

Nick fished the credit card out of his wallet and handed it to him. "Something like that." Covering the cost of settling Buddy and Dunk in was getting to be an expensive business. They'd been at the farm for almost two weeks and already he'd spent far more than he had planned. Still, if it paved the way for getting past the mile-high wall Vicky put up between them, it'd be well worth it at twice the price. No one expected redemption to come cheap.

It being Tuesday, the supply store wasn't especially busy, so Wally leaned against the counter as if settling in for a long chat. "She carries a lot of pain around. Still. Hides it well, though. Keeps up a good front for Taylor and all. But there's a deep wound that ain't close to healed."

Rather deep thoughts for the likes of a scruffy old guy in flannel and denim. Then again, Nick supposed some people could think of him as a scruffy not-so-old guy in flannel and denim. But where Wally had a settled warmth about him, Nick felt as if he bumbled through life one misstep at a time. Buddy and Dunk—and the relationship he was counting on them to help fix—were the first steps out of that grim existence. He wondered if the two animals knew just how much he was banking on them. Everybody in this whole situation seemed the most unlikely of characters—was it a fool notion to think it could ever meet with success?

Wally gave a low whistle as he handed back the sizable receipt. "You're puttin' a lot into this. But I admire a man who doesn't back down from an uphill battle."

Nick gave a low laugh of his own. "Uphill battle about covers it. With Vicky, I mean. Taylor's a sweet little guy. Treats me like I had nothing to do with his father's death."

Nick stopped short, nearly gulping back the words he hadn't intended to say out loud. He wiped his hands down his face and shifted his feet, wincing at the exposed feeling the words evoked. Guilt was a sly thing, creeping up on a soul without warning and in the worst places. Grief, too. After all, Nick had lost his best friend. He'd discovered the one-two punch could bring a man to his knees.

"That how you feel?" Wally asked. Nick was grateful to hear no judgment in the man's tone.

It took him a moment to answer. "What does it matter how I feel? It's what she thinks."

"It is," Wally replied. "What a lot of folks around here think, I expect."

If there was anything Nick knew for certain, it was that a

lot of people blamed him for Roger's death. Including himself. The pile of paperwork and policy-citing from the Department of Fish and Wildlife hadn't done much to change that. Nick wasn't sure it ever would. The only opinions he cared much about now were Vicky's and Taylor's.

"Changing it is gonna be hard. It'll take time. More than a couple of weeks, I expect. You've had experience with animals like Buddy and Dunk, so I gather you're a patient man. Stubborn, too."

When had a trip to the supply store come with a dose of philosophy like this? "You think she'll come 'round?" It surprised him how much he needed to know if Wally thought it was possible. After all, the man who delivered a stern lecture to him a handful of days ago now was acting like he might be on Nick's side. And he could very much use an ally right about now.

Wally scratched his chin. "I think she needs to."

That wasn't a prediction if she would, but it was close enough to encouragement that Nick took it. "I need her to," he admitted, again wondering how the conversation had gone so deep in the checkout aisle next to garden gloves and batteries.

He *did* need her to. It was why he hadn't flinched at the costs and the effort involved in rehabilitating Buddy and Dunk. This was about more than just a horse and a donkey finding their way into a better world.

"You a praying man?" Wally asked. "I saw you in church on Sunday."

Nick could guess what Wally was hinting at—just being inside a church wasn't the same thing as having faith.

Roger had been a praying man. He had talked about praying for his wife and unborn son. Nick just sort of sopped it up by proximity. Nick easily held the idea of a

God who cared, just not the idea of a God who cared for someone like him. It had to go both ways, didn't it? He didn't think his indifference earned him much in the way of grace. Not after what he'd done—or more precisely, what he'd failed to do. That whole "If I could trade places" thing? The irrational notion that things would be so much better if he'd caught that poacher's bullet and not Roger? It nipped at his heels every time he looked at Taylor's eyes and saw Roger's gaze looking back at him. Or caught Vicky's glare and felt the gaping hole Roger's death left in her life.

Wally gave a gruff sound and Nick realized he hadn't yet answered the man's prying question. "Not especially." While that felt like a dodge, neither yes or no seemed to fit, either.

Wally gave another gruff sound. The man seemed to have an endless vocabulary of snorts, grunts, and huffs that were a surprisingly effective means of communication. *Rather like horses*, Nick thought to himself and almost broke out in a laugh.

"Might be time to start." Wally said it as if it were as easy as adding a pack of gum to his current purchase.

"Doesn't really work that way, does it?" Nick asked.

"Sure it does. Nothing fancy needed. Some days I don't even bother with words."

Nick could just imagine the Almighty trying to work out Wally's symphony of sounds. Oddly enough, it was encouraging. As if it wasn't such a ridiculous thing that he'd felt a bit of comfort sitting in the very back pew of church on Sunday. As if maybe it was just the right thing to buy Taylor those boots. As if it might have been the thing God had in mind.

And if that didn't boggle the mind, Nick didn't know what did.

"Maybe I will," he found himself saying.

"Maybe you should," Wally replied, and some of the stern tone returned to his voice. Nick began to feel Wally would ask him about it the next time he came into the store.

Nick gave a nod. Why not try prayer? After all, he needed all the help he could get on this particular uphill climb.

And so it was that Nick Youngston attempted his first prayer in decades—maybe even his first ever—in a truck traveling down the road toward the sisters' farm.

Show me how. Help me do right by them. Heal what You can, and help me live with the scars.

He managed those words, but discovered he resorted to what surely must have sounded like Wally's grunts and groans by the end.

Was it a prayer? By Wally's standards, Nick guessed it was.

Hopefully, God agreed. And listened.

Chapter Six

Wednesday was the last day of the school year, and a booth inside the Sundial diner was a collection of giggles, crayons, smiles, and mess. What else could it be with four small children and three moms gathered for a celebratory end-of-year lunch? Between the grilled cheese sandwiches, BLTs, and baby food, Vicky, Meg, and Carly laughed about the challenges of motherhood, encouraged each other for the summer to come, and tried to stay ahead of the crazy mess the four children made at the table. Even though Meg ran the diner, she gave herself the gift of this meal once every few weeks, and Vicky knew it was as much of a lifeline for the two other mothers as it was for her.

With one exception.

Try as she might, Vicky's heart still pinched at the fact that both the women sitting with her had found love and a partner to share the burden of parenthood. She was happy for both of them—she really was—but she was starting to miss the camaraderie of having another mother who was still "going this alone."

Five-month-old Anson had just started eating simple foods, and Meg's twin girls took endless delight in watching Carly feed the baby. Taylor was more interested in drawing on the paper place mats with the jar of crayons set in the middle of the table. Vicky rarely recognized what Taylor drew, but always praised whatever her son said the picture was. More often than not these days, it was a horse. Or a donkey. It was impossible to tell unless Taylor named them.

Her son remained fixated on the barnyard pair. In fact, he'd worn his barn boots to school today, again. She was glad the barn boots hadn't made it to the *actual* barn yet, because as soon as they did, they'd surely be too dirty to wear at school, church, or other places. The way Taylor kept asking, she wouldn't be able to put off another visit to the farm to see Dunk and Buddy for much longer. Professionally, she owed the pair a visit to assess their health, but she was putting it off.

"Whatcha drawing, Taylor?" Meg's youngest daughter, Tabitha, asked as she pointed to a gray blob with what Vicky could only guess was four legs and a tail. Near as she could tell, the gray blobs were Dunk, the brown ones Buddy.

"Dunk," Taylor replied.

"I see him out my bedroom window every day," Tabitha's sister Sadie offered. "He's funny."

"I wanna see Dunk again," Taylor said. Actually, whined was closer to the truth. Taylor had asked to go over to the Three Sisters Farm so many times since Sunday it was beginning to grate on Vicky's nerves. *This is what preschoolers do*, she reminded herself. *Someday I'll find his persistence a good quality.* Today, not so much.

"You'll get a chance," Meg assured the boy. "He's not going anywhere so he'll always be there ready for you to visit now that's school's done." Meg gave Vicky a knowing glance, a signal that she knew it was really Vicky who needed to be ready to visit. Losing her first husband to an accident in the Air Force, Meg understood the emotional black hole of blame and how it affected a young widow.

"How 'bout I draw you standing next to Dunk?" Sadie suggested, picking up a blue crayon. "In your new blue boots?"

Taylor instantly agreed, and things hummed along happily for the next few minutes as Vicky and Meg offered Carly encouragement that one day she would sleep through the night again. "Just not anytime soon," Vicky managed with a chuckle. Anson's teething was causing Carly and Jack a string of sleepless nights. Vicky could sympathize; Taylor had been a notoriously bad sleeper, which had made single parenthood a long, dark trial in the early months. Even while Vicky offered sincere encouragement to Carly, the inward thought of *at least you're not alone* pinched Vicky's heart.

I'm not really alone, Vicky tried to remind herself as she gazed around the table. *It just feels like it sometimes.* She tried to shake off the melancholy thought and enjoy the company of good friends and joyful children.

That joy came to a halt when halfway through a conversation about baby foods, Vicky looked up to see Nick walk in the diner.

It was going to happen eventually. High Mountain wasn't a large town, and she'd be running into Nick often, whether she liked it or not. Only their mutual avoidance had kept it from happening more often in the few weeks he'd been here. The look Meg shot her when Nick walked in told Vicky that her friend understood things.

Still, he had been kind to Taylor. He'd bought him the boots her son absolutely adored. And he'd been respectful of her as Taylor's mom and as someone who had a lot of emotions to work through where he was concerned.

It'd be so much easier if he was awful, Vicky thought. *He won't seem to stay the terrible person I've built him up to be in my mind.* She didn't know what to do about that. She resisted the idea that God might be nudging her toward a forgiveness she was not ready to extend. Exactly how does one get ready to forgive? Or is it always a question of never being ready and forgiving anyway?

Interrupting her thoughts, Taylor lit up the moment he saw Nick. "Horsey Man!" he shouted loudly. Her son waved so enthusiastically that Vicky barely saved his milk from toppling over and dousing the table.

"Hey there, Taylor," Nick called. He always seemed so happy at Taylor's greetings. *It would also help if he weren't quite so handsome,* Vicky added wryly to herself. *He grins when he sees Taylor, and you probably frown when you see him,* Vicky thought as she forced a smile to her face.

"Does he always call you Horsey Man?" Tabitha asked, clearly finding the title amusing.

"Seems so," Nick answered, not looking the least bit bothered by it. Had he possessed that almost-charming, self-effacing grin when he'd been Roger's friend? "Kind of getting used to it, actually."

Used to it. The nature of the phrase bothered her. Anything that hinted of Nick staying here for a long time or being involved in her life rubbed Vicky the wrong way. That wasn't fair—or gracious—but since when did emotions follow any rules?

Meg seemed to decide a conversation was needed. "Okay, kiddos, lunch is over. Gather up your stuff so you can all meet the sitter at the park with Carly and Anson. Us moms have things to do."

The three moms had come up with the idea to combine their different babysitting needs to create a full-time position for one dear woman from the church. Their schedules often meshed easily, so the setup was one of the great blessings of Vicky's life. Dependable and loving child care made a lot of things possible, especially for a single mom.

"Can we talk?" Nick asked.

Vicky watched Nick wait patiently while the parade of children, strollers, and backpacks headed out the diner door. He turned back after they left, offering that same apologetic grin. "A lot going on there."

"All the time," she replied, wishing there wasn't so much weariness in her reply.

He raised an eyebrow in a silent request to sit down opposite her, and she nodded to him. He paused for a moment before asking, "It's hard, isn't it?" His voice was low and somber. It let her know Nick recognized the weight of her burden.

"Almost always," she said.

There was another pause before he said, "I wish every single day that weren't so." His words came awkwardly, but with sincerity.

"Me, too." The admission settled quietly in the air between them. Vicky supposed that if there was anything they were in agreement about, it was the mountain of regret they both had over that day. Different reasons, and she would argue different burdens of guilt, but there was more than enough regret to go around.

Meg silently set a cup of coffee in front of Nick. She nodded to both of them, leaving them alone. He'd clearly come to say something—the determination was written all over his face.

Nick cleared his throat. "I want to talk about Taylor and Dunk and Buddy."

That wasn't hard to guess. They didn't have any other

mutual topic of conversation except for Roger, and she hoped he wasn't foolish enough to try and have any conversation about Roger here in the diner. She wasn't ready to have that conversation anywhere, much less in the center of High Mountain's gossip chain. "What about them?"

He held the white stoneware cup of coffee but didn't take a sip. And he didn't meet her eyes. "We need to be careful."

"How so?" She surprised herself by wanting to hear his thoughts.

"Buddy and Dunk are making great strides. Really, I hadn't expected them to adjust as well as they have. In fact, I think we can bring the farrier in next week."

They'd had conversations with the three sisters about needing to get the animals used to basic levels of human touch so that they could receive the care they needed. They'd been neglected so long that they viewed most interactions with people as threats. Vicky had been forced to be extremely cautious just to get simple care tasks done, and many of the things she would have liked to do to assess the animals had not been done yet for fear of how Dunk and Buddy might react.

This was one place where Vicky had to admit Nick possessed a gift. He seemed especially good at connecting with the pair, at gaining their trust and reducing their fears. Buddy and Dunk had made impressive strides in only two weeks, and she could not deny that the progress lay with Nick's talent for reaching them.

"That's good," Vicky had to admit.

"Dunk's hooves are a real problem," Nick said.

It was true. The poor donkey's hooves had gone untended for so long they'd begun to curl grotesquely upward. Taylor thought they looked like elf shoes—which might have been amusing had they not been irritating the donkey's foot so severely that they caused him to walk improperly. He could not run and was likely in pain.

Nick knew the severity of the situation as well. "Ticks me off how they've gone so long without care," he said. "Their lives are going to be a thousand percent better at the farm."

"I agree." She couldn't seem to push herself beyond two-word responses.

"That parade thing the sisters are talking about, though? I don't know. Noise, crowds, distractions. I'd have reservations about an animal I trusted joining in, much less one facing the readjustment Dunk and Buddy are."

"That's true."

"I know I may have put the idea in Taylor's head of riding them. That was a mistake. I was trying for something special for the little guy, and I reached too far."

Vicky absolutely agreed. But she tried not to let her reply sound harsh, even though she suspected it did.

In fact, it had been bothering her that she didn't put a stop to the risky idea the moment Nick suggested it. Taylor was too young, and the animals were way too unpredictable. It had almost no hope of being safe. Taylor's near obsession with the idea had been the only thing keeping her from an outright no. *I should have said no right away.* Nick's admission of just wanting to reach for something special rang too true to her. It was she herself who hadn't been able to shut the idea down. What was it that she was thinking earlier about there being more than enough regret to go around?

Vicky was just about to voice her opinion that they should put a stop to the whole idea when Nick said, "So I think we need a plan B if it's not safe for Taylor to ride either of them."

If? She thought Taylor would be fortunate to get a chance to ride either animal within the quiet context of the farm, much less the commotion of a parade. Even with Nick's gifts, Vicky didn't see much chance at all of Taylor being in the parade the way he wanted. His clear love for the idea didn't overcome the enormous risk.

They were almost in agreement on this. So why did his use of the word "we" stick in her craw so much?

"I know how much he wants to," Nick went on, sounding genuinely heartsick about it. "I'm not sure what you think we ought to do."

Again with the "we." Much as she didn't want to acknowledge, they were in this together. He'd shown up in High Mountain and thrust this into her life. She had the sense, as she'd had many times since he walked up to her in the park two weeks ago, that this was about way more than a horse, a donkey, and a little boy.

Vicky fixed Nick with a steady gaze. "I need to be absolutely sure Taylor is safe. And you're right, the parade may not be the place where that can happen."

Nick shrugged. "But it might. Those two have shown amazing progress. However, the comfort of the barn is a lot different than the commotion of a parade. Dunk is fine with the dogs around him, so that's a good sign, but Buddy is still agitated."

"It's Dunk that Taylor wants to ride."

Nick gave a small laugh. "So I've noticed. They connect, those two. I've seen that kind of thing before, but never in someone that young. I think Dunk is a special animal. And I'm glad for it, because Buddy has a longer way to go."

Vicky had seen a dynamic like that before. Pairs, or even litters of animals, where one rebounded so much easier than others. They were like people in that way—wounded by trauma in different ways and recovering with just as much variety.

"Youth brings resilience." The Fish and Wildlife office had given her access to a grief counselor, and it was one of the first things the woman had said. It was something Vicky held on to when she worried that Taylor would carry deep scars over what had happened to his father.

"It does," he agreed. "Those of us who aren't quite so young just have to slog along until it hurts less, I suppose."

There it was again. The double-edged sword of her attitude toward Nick. He had deep grief, too. Under circumstances that wounded him as well. But she would never equate it to what she and Taylor had lost. *Your pain will never be bigger and deeper than mine.* It seemed such a petty, graceless thought to have.

Nick cleared his throat, making Vicky wonder if her thoughts showed on her face. "So what I'm hoping, if it's okay with you, is that Taylor spends time with Dunk. Buddy will be nearby—those two need each other and separating them won't be a good idea for a while—but I think Taylor's connection with Dunk can help."

Vicky raised an eyebrow. "You want to borrow my son as a donkey rehabilitation program?"

Nick laughed out loud. He had one of those deep and hearty laughs. Roger told her he was always looking for ways to make Nick bust out laughing for the sheer fun of it. Nick shook his head before replying, "Yeah, I suppose I am."

She had to ask. "You didn't plan it this way? Set this all up?"

Nick's face was a mixture of expressions. "Not this. I mean, I did hope bringing Buddy and Dunk here might mean we could begin to…talk…but I hadn't planned on the way Taylor and Dunk connect. I haven't pushed it or done anything to manufacture it, if that's what you mean."

She lowered a suspicious eyebrow. "The boots?"

"Were just a gift," he insisted. "An impulse. Honest."

Vicky hesitated. Not because she didn't believe Nick, but because she did. Her stalwart resistance to him and his motives was starting to fray around the edges. Now who was being a stubborn donkey?

"I just wanted to give the little guy something." Nick looked down at his coffee for a moment before returning his gaze to Vicky. When he did, there was a stunning sorrow in his eyes. "Because I took so much from him."

Suddenly she heard herself saying, "I need to stop by the farm tomorrow afternoon. How about I bring Taylor along with me?"

Nick smiled. Not a wide, victorious grin, but a quiet, careful, grateful smile.

She tried not to be surprised when she found herself smiling back.

Chapter Seven

"Dump it into the pail," Nick coached as he handed the scoop of feed to Taylor the following afternoon.

"It's lunchtime," Taylor said as he followed Nick's directions. It took both hands for Taylor to hold the scoop and tilt its contents into the white plastic pail Nick was holding.

Task completed, Taylor turned in Dunk's direction and began braying like a donkey. Loudly. Well, sort of like a donkey. The small voice and high pitch didn't quite match Dunk's bray. In fact, it made Nick wince a bit.

"I'm telling him it's lunchtime," Taylor announced. Taylor had been "telling" Dunk things since his arrival on the farm. The little guy considered himself fluent in Donkey. It had been amusing the first time. Nick had to admit it was getting tiresome. Whatever folks said about the terrible twos must apply doubly to three-year-olds as well.

Dunk, however, seemed to enjoy it. The donkey's ears shifted immediately toward Taylor. He brayed back, sending Taylor into a fit of giggles. "See?" Taylor said. "We talk!"

While horses could have notoriously delicate stomachs, donkeys weren't so discriminating. Which made it useful to feed the pair separately but near each other. Cay was coaxing Buddy to eat his meal while Taylor and Nick did so for Dunk.

Taylor banged against the bucket Nick was holding so that it rattled with the feed and brayed again. Dunk replied, and began walking over to where they were standing. Out of the corner of his eye, Nick saw Buddy watch, then lower his head into the bucket hung at his end of the stall. *There you go, Buddy. Take your cue from Dunk and Taylor. You've got friends here.*

Nick gave Taylor a pat on the back as Dunk ducked his nose into the bucket. Carefully, Nick laid a hand on the side of Dunk's neck, letting him slowly adjust to the touch. *Touch = food = good.* They were rewiring Dunk's attitude one meal at a time, and it was working even better and faster than Nick had expected.

He heard footsteps in the straw behind him and turned to see Vicky come into the barn. She'd been helping her mom, Barb, get Daisy the dog adjusted to her new, larger wheels and harness. A pack of puppies had been the first animals to launch Three Sisters Rescue Farm, and one of the beagle-mix puppies had needed the canine equivalent of a wheelchair to get around.

Taylor chose to greet his mother with yet another loud, enthusiastic donkey bray. Vicky's slight wince told Nick she'd been enduring quite a lot of braying lately. It really was adorable…until it wasn't. He'd only been here less than an hour, but he suspected Taylor brayed all day.

"How's Daisy liking her new wheels?" he asked as Taylor continued to bray.

"Took to them like a pro. She's an amazing dog." Vicky had a nice smile. It was a shame the world didn't see it more often. Somewhere in the corner of his mind, he found himself wondering if he'd ever live to see her smile at him.

The continual sour frown she wore around him at first had softened. A bit. Now it was closer to a resigned tolerance. Possibly only for Taylor's sake.

He shouldn't expect more. Except that he found himself hoping for more. Hoping that somehow, with the help of these two remarkable animals, she might stop viewing him as the man who destroyed her family. He wanted that for himself as much as for her. *Everybody in this barn is trying to pull themselves back out from a wounded place. Could You help us help each other?* Nick was stunned to discover thoughts were actually an easy prayer. After all, if there ever was a situation where the power of the Almighty was needed, it felt like this one.

Dunk joined in braying with Taylor, and the loud racket pulled Nick from his thoughts and made both he and Vicky cringe.

"Does your mom tell you not to talk with your mouth full?" he asked Taylor, shouting above the noise but taking care to keep his voice playful.

"Yep," Taylor replied.

"How about we teach Dunk that. No talking while you eat. It's a good rule for people as well as donkeys, don't you think?"

Taylor considered this with an adorable seriousness. Nick's affection for the boy was growing by leaps and bounds. If this setup didn't repair things between himself, Taylor, and Vicky, it was going to leave a gaping hole in his life when it came time to leave High Mountain and return to whatever job would be waiting for him at the wildlife service.

Who was he kidding? His life had been one giant gaping hole since Roger's death. Not as big as the hole in Vicky's and Taylor's. But big enough to make a man rescue two animals and bring them here. Talk about your outrageous plans…

Both boy and donkey settled down. The barn's sudden quiet was a welcome thing indeed.

"Do donkeys have inside voices?" Vicky asked Nick. There was something almost like a smile in her eyes.

"Not that I'm aware of," he replied. It felt close to a joke. A lighthearted exchange. *Tiny steps forward.* He looked down at Taylor. "But I've heard little boys do."

"Mom tells me to use mine. A lot."

Nick hunched down to Taylor's height. Something about interacting with the boy on this level—even though his knee groaned when he did—dug deep into his heart. After all, Taylor looked at him without any of the emotional baggage that always lurked behind Vicky's eyes. Nick liked being the Horsey Man very much.

"Inside voices are good," he replied. "Outside voices are good, too, but you gotta save them for outside."

"But we *are* outside," Taylor protested.

Were all preschoolers so good at asking questions? A long-suffering expression rose up in Vicky's features, and Nick had a new appreciation for the demands of parenting.

"We need to teach Buddy and Dunk they can be calm and happy here. Just like you. You like it here, right?"

Taylor nodded with a sweet grin.

I like it here, too, Nick thought.

"You might like it even more to know Grannie and Auntie Cay have cookies in the kitchen," Vicky suggested. "They're waiting for you."

With that invitation, Taylor sped off in the direction of the big white house. It seemed like one of those quintessential family farmhouses, full of good memories and love. A part of him wondered what it would be like to be invited in there someday. High Mountain was supposed to be a temporary stay, but he was starting to think of the place as a very nice town to call home.

That wasn't a smart idea. The most he could ever hope for here was to make things right. Hoping for more seemed too irrational, even for the Almighty to consider. In this case, peace and happiness were two different goals. He could get to one, but he wasn't at all sure the other was waiting for him here.

"How is Buddy's anxiety level?" Vicky asked, the clinical expression returning to her voice.

He matched her informational tone. "Still high. But it definitely has come down, near as I can tell. I wouldn't want to separate him from Dunk or put him in with any other animals. The dogs still make him skittish. But he ate well this morning, and he let me touch his fetlock on the front legs."

Vicky nodded, casting her gaze over Dunk to where Buddy was standing at the far end of the pen. "Does he ever come over?"

"To people, you mean? No, we mostly have to approach him. He'll come up to the fence if Dunk is here, but he stays back there when people are around. He's stopped pacing, though, so that's good."

"How long will it take, you think, for them to adjust?"

Was she asking how long he would be around? How much longer she would have to endure his presence?

"Hard to say. You know these things never go in straight lines. One step forward, two steps back, then three forward." Nick felt as if he were answering on both fronts—the animals and the people. The duality of the truth made him feel a bit dizzy.

"That's how these things go." She paused for a long moment as they each watched Buddy and Dunk. Both animals had such expressive eyes. It made Nick wonder if they had any idea of their role here. The old "who rescued who?" might very well apply.

There didn't seem to be any need to fill the silence. The barn was a big and enveloping space, bright from the clear mountain sunshine and yet somehow cozy. Cay had often said how much she liked to spend time here, and he could easily see why.

"When I'm ready…" she began, giving a soft sigh instead of finishing the thought. She put her hands on the pen fencing as if to steady herself.

He turned to look at her, daring to meet her gaze. Roger had always said Vicky's face could say a million things without saying a word, and it was certainly true now. He gave her the gift of silence to finish her thought because it was so clear she had more to say.

"When I'm ready," she repeated, a bit more strength to her voice. She looked away just then, as if she couldn't be facing him while she said the next part. "I want to hear what happened. In your words."

There was no question what she was referring to. She was asking him to recount the worst day of his life. The incident that had taken Roger's life. The circumstances he had allowed to take Roger's life.

There were official records. Departmental reports, inquiry assessments, factual recounts. That wasn't what Vicky was asking. She was asking him for his version of the story.

And Nick knew, just by the look in her eyes, that she was well aware of what it would cost him to tell it. What it would cost both of them.

"When you're ready to hear it," he replied. It occurred to

him that he might never know if he'd be ready. Then again, wasn't it part of why he came here? To cleanse that wound?

Her hands tightened their grip on the rail. Nick could almost feel the battle in her—after all, he waged a version of it in himself.

"I'm not ready. Not yet."

Me neither, Nick thought. And as he stared at Buddy, watching and listening from his distance at the far side of the pen, he added, *None of us are.*

Vicky loved her aunts. Her mother and the two other McNally sisters were a fine model of what family could be. She had all the support she could ever need from these three women, and she was grateful for it.

Most days.

Then there were times like this one, where it felt as if she had three mothers. Three nosy, privacy invading, opinion declaring, coming-close-to-smothering mothers.

And today all of them wanted to know what she was going to do about Nick.

Even I don't know what I'm going to do about Nick, she wanted to shout.

The four of them—Vicky, her mother, Aunt Cay, and Aunt Peggy—were supposedly in the farmhouse kitchen to make preparations for a family supper. Supposedly, because no one seemed to be doing anything but watch Nick as he worked on the new fence for Buddy and Dunk.

"It's going to be a fine fence," Aunt Peggy said.

"All that hard work for free," Aunt Cay said. "It's a blessing."

Nick had been in town for two weeks, and everyone's opinion of the man seemed to be shifting away from the villain Vicky had painted him as. He was not a blessing—

well, at least not to her. He was an irritant. A reminder. Something poking at her in uncomfortable ways.

"Taylor gets such a kick out of Dunk," her mother said with a chuckle.

"And Dunk seems to get such a kick out of Taylor," replied Aunt Peggy. "That donkey sure lights up when Taylor is around. Not even Tabitha and Sadie can get that kind of reaction out of him."

"Maybe it's all the braying," Vicky said wearily.

"He's still doing that?" Aunt Peggy asked.

"Oh, he's still doing that," Vicky replied. "All the time. Why couldn't he have been as excited about the rabbits? They're quiet."

"When we first got the dogs, I thought I'd be hearing puppies yapping in my sleep," Aunt Cay offered. "Actually I *did* hear puppies yapping in my sleep. When I *got* sleep. Which seemed like never." She gave Vicky a sympathetic look. "Young ones of any type can be a challenge."

All the sisters—who had once been young mothers, but none had ever been a young single mom—made little *hmms* and ohs, yeses, and other noises of agreement.

Then they went back to staring out the window at Nick. As if it were fascinating entertainment instead of just a man going through the motions of digging fencepost holes.

Of course, it was her mother who could no longer resist and addressed the elephant in the room. "You know, he's not so bad."

Vicky had little chance of dodging the subject, but it was worth a try. She offered her mother a conciliatory smile. "No, Dunk isn't as much of a challenge as I feared. In fact, he's adjusting better than Buddy. That will work in your favor."

Mom was undeterred. "I meant Nick."

It took a moment for Vicky to decide how to answer that. "He's been very nice to Taylor."

"Those blue boots are adorable," Aunt Peggy cooed. "I don't think I've seen him without them on since."

Vicky made herself smile. "Yes, I've had a blue-hoofed donkey in my house ever since."

Cay shook her head. "Grant had a fixation with bears one winter back when he was about Taylor's age. Sometimes I wonder if that's where his big bear of a personality set in."

All the women laughed. Vicky's big, tall cousin was very bearlike in his ways—before Meg. Now he was a little more teddy bear than grizzly bear, but not completely. It was again a reminder of how a second chance at love had changed Grant's and Meg's world. And that of their daughters. Vicky said a small prayer that there would come a time when happy endings like that wouldn't pinch her spirit the way they did now.

"Are you going to talk to him about it?" Mom asked, pulling Vicky from her thoughts.

"About what?" Vicky asked, even though she knew it was a pointless question.

"About Roger. About what happened."

Even though she'd told Nick she would ask him about it when she was ready, Vicky felt just a bit cornered by the question. After all, she didn't know when she'd be ready, or even how to get ready. So much pain was involved. Suppressed pain—how could a young single mother function otherwise?—but pain nonetheless.

"That's going to be a hard conversation," she admitted.

"Yes, it will," Aunt Cay conceded. "But it's why he's here, you know."

Again, Vicky felt the hint of manipulation she'd been

fighting at Nick showing up with rescue animals and being so kind to Taylor. He kept saying he was here to set things right, but to her it seemed too much like he was here to make her hear his side of the story and forgive him. She felt as reluctant to do that as Buddy was reluctant to come out from his corner of the pen. "I know that's why he said he was here."

"I mean more than that," Aunt Cay went on. "You know I think none of our animals come to us by accident. God sends 'em. Seems to me that applies to humans, too."

"God did not send Nick Youngston."

Mom put her hand on Vicky's. "Honey, you've been through a terrible loss. And you've been so strong for Taylor. But you're not okay. You've been lugging around a big load of anger and pain. You're exhausted. Don't you think maybe God might be giving you a chance to lay it all down?"

The deep truth of her mother's words brought a lump to Vicky's throat. It was so much easier to carry the hurt around than to do the hard work of healing. It seemed as if it would take so much more strength than she had. "It's too soon," she nearly whimpered, feeling ashamed at sounding as weak as she felt.

Mom pulled her into a hug, and her two aunts moved from their places by the window to join in. It took all of Vicky's strength not to cry. "I don't think it's too soon," Mom said. "God's timing is never wrong, even when you feel like it is."

"We'll be backing you up the whole time," Aunt Peggy said. "In prayer, hugs, watching Taylor, or whatever else you need." Her aunt gave her hand a tight squeeze. "Nick won't be here forever. Don't let this chance get past you just because it's scary. Do it for Taylor if not for yourself."

Vicky wondered if Aunt Peggy knew she was saying the one thing that would convince her.

"You don't have to settle things now," Aunt Cay said. "At least make sure he finishes the fence first, just in case it all goes sideways."

Aunt Peggy poked Aunt Cay in the arm, and for a moment there was a glimpse of the wild trio the sisters had been as young girls. "You don't mean that." Aunt Cay was the last person in the world to get so transactional about something so personal.

"Of course I don't," Aunt Cay assured. "But I am really happy for the new fence. When Buddy finally finds his courage, we're gonna need it."

When Buddy finally finds his courage. When would she find hers? Vicky looked out the window, still in the middle of her aunts, and felt a new affinity for the wounded, frightened horse.

Nick seemed to be a master of saving animals from their troubled pasts. He certainly had a talent for connecting with them. Dunk already trusted Nick, as did Taylor.

Could she get to the point where she trusted him, too?

Chapter Eight

Vicky's office assistant, Gloria, poked her head into the examination room from the hallway on Friday around lunchtime. "That's the last appointment. What a morning!"

Some days went along at a pleasant pace at the veterinary clinic. But Fridays could often be a whirlwind of emergencies and crises. The elder dog with a concerning snakebite. The cat that had swallowed a length of gift ribbon. The young puppy that wouldn't eat. And Mrs. Northrup, who seemed to think something was wrong with her cat nearly every week, even though Vicky rarely found any reason for concern. Some days Vicky wondered if Mrs. Northrup just wanted somewhere to go and someone to talk to. Surely there were less expensive ways to find company. She made a note to see if her aunts could get her into one of the church bible studies. If she'd leave Custard alone for two hours on a Wednesday morning.

"Let's close up for lunch break," she instructed Gloria as she checked her watch. "I'm ten minutes late as it is." The moms had decided that the school break merited another round of lunch at the Sundial, and Vicky readily agreed.

"Got it. See you later."

Just as Vicky grabbed her handbag and headed for the door to dash down the sidewalk to the Sundial, her phone buzzed with a text. It was probably Meg or Carly asking if she'd be arriving soon—they were always gracious with how unpredictable her schedule could be.

But the text was not from any of the moms. It was a photo. An image of Buddy came up on her screen. It took her a second to notice that the horse was not in the far corner as he'd been for so long, but a few yards toward the center of the pen.

He'd come forward.

Progress was the text from Nick.

She couldn't help but smile. She was rooting for the beleaguered pair. Not just for them, or for another success for Three Sisters Farm, but for Taylor, too. How he'd come to be so invested in the horse and donkey, she couldn't say.

Actually, she could.

Nick.

This progress was Nick's victory as much as it was Buddy's. She had to admire how he'd been patient with Buddy, using the bond the horse had with his braver donkey companion to convince him his new home was safe. This victory, along with dozens of other actions large and small, kept nudging her to the same challenging notion: Nick Youngston was not the villain she'd made him out to be.

Or, at least, he *might not be* the villain she'd made him out to be. Was she ready to consider that? Ready, as her mother said yesterday, to lay down that heavy burden of anger she'd been carrying around? Maybe it wasn't just the horses who needed to show a little courage in High Mountain.

"Mommy!" Taylor called when Vicky walked into the diner to see the whole lunch group waiting. His cheerful voice warmed her heart. The whole world brightened with his sunny smile. He was the light of her life. "Can I have grilled cheese?" he asked. "And pickles?"

Taylor loved pickles as much as cookies or ice cream. No matter what the main course, pickles were always a requisite side dish.

"Sounds good to me." She slid into the booth next to her son and accepted a delightfully squishy kiss. Taylor was always the best antidote to all the world's complexities. Vicky looked at him. "Can I have a tuna melt? With fruit salad?" she teased.

For as much as Taylor found pickles delicious, he found tuna fish yucky. His face scrunched up in revulsion. "Icky fish."

"You never know, young man," Carly remarked with a grin. "Someday you may think tuna fish is terrific."

Taylor made a face that caused the whole table to laugh. Meg took everyone's order back to the kitchen and then returned to the table. "How's Anson doing?" she asked Carly. "Are you happy with that new therapy?"

The baby's spina bifida gave him some physical challenges, but for the most part he had done remarkably well. "His motor skills seem to be improving. They're telling Jack and me that his walking should only be slightly impaired, if at all."

"Hooray for Anson!" Tabitha cheered. "He's gonna be amazing."

Vicky smiled at the baby boy. "I think Anson's already amazing, don't you?" she replied to the girls. They both readily agreed, and Sadie gave the baby a kiss on his chubby elbow. There was a lot of love around this table.

"Speaking of amazing steps," Meg said as she returned from the kitchen to join the table for lunch, "Did you hear the news from the farm?"

The girls looked as if they would bust—clearly they'd been waiting for Vicky to arrive to announce what she already knew. Taylor's eyes were wide with interest. "What?" he nearly shouted.

"I've even got a photo," Vicky announced. "Want to see?" Pulling the photo up on her phone, she showed it to the children. "See where he is?"

"See that?" Tabitha asked Taylor. "He's out from the corner! Look at him out from there!"

"Buddy is the hero of the day," Meg said.

"Yay!" Taylor cheered. "Hooray for Buddy!"

Meg's raised eyebrow hinted at what Vicky was trying not to think. That the victory wasn't solely Buddy's. "That's faster than you expected, isn't it?"

"Much." Why was it so hard to admit that Nick had done wonders with the horse?

"Mr. Nick is really good at that, isn't he?" Sadie asked.

There seemed little point in denying it. "Yes, he seems to have a real gift."

"I like the Horsey Man," Taylor declared. As if it were that simple. To him, Vicky supposed, it was. "Do you think he likes pickles?"

He had no idea what a loaded question that was. Roger liked pickles—not that she thought such a thing was inherited. A memory of Roger dipping his finger in the pickle jar and presenting his pickle-juice finger to baby Taylor flooded her memory. Taylor's reaction was a comical face she could recall to this day. She wondered if Roger had somehow imbued his fondness for pickles in his son that day. It felt wrong to let Taylor share that with anyone else.

"Probably not as much as you," she managed to reply. So many little details would snag her spirit lately. Things were surfacing from the place she'd kept them so tightly locked.

"*Nobody* likes pickles as much as you," Tabitha said dramatically.

Except your father, Vicky added in her mind.

All through lunch, Taylor brought up the Horsey Man over and over. He talked about Buddy and Dunk, reminding everyone how much he wanted to ride Dunk in the upcoming parade. Everyone—except her, that is—took Buddy's big advancement as a sign that it would happen. Vicky began to feel boxed in by the only two possible outcomes: Nick would succeed and Taylor would get his wish, or Nick would fail and Taylor would be crushed. Both held huge consequences.

At one point the constant talk of Nick and Buddy and Dunk became too much, and Vicky excused herself to go hide in the ladies' room. It was childish, she knew, but life was so overwhelming lately.

She wasn't completely surprised that Meg found a way to come join her. "You okay?" she asked in a voice filled with understanding.

"I should be," was all Vicky could think of to say.

Meg leaned against the sink. "This is hard stuff. For you, and probably for him, too."

Vicky didn't like to think of this as hard for Nick. It made him too human. Wounded like her. The way she thought about him was changing in ways that made her wildly uncomfortable.

"Are you going to go there? Talk to him about what happened to Roger?" That was Meg. Kind, compassionate, but direct as the day was long.

"I probably should." That felt like the most dangerous of admissions. If she did talk to Nick about that terrible day, she might have to change how she viewed it. But she wasn't sure she could do that.

"You probably should. I don't think Cay is wrong. I think Nick is here for a reason. And it's not Buddy or Dunk. Well, it's not *just* Buddy or Dunk."

Nick watched in quiet amazement as Buddy took another step. The horse would come as far as the center of the pen now when people came around. He'd been there four times so far today—a place he'd not come near since the day Nick had brought him to Three Sisters Rescue Farm. Those twenty-odd feet were the longest distance in the world—for both of them.

Maybe the only longer distance in his life right now was the distance between him and Vicky. It struck him—not for the first time—that Vicky and Taylor were the human versions of Buddy and Dunk. Both wounded, but emerging from those wounds in drastically different ways. Taylor with Dunk's amiablc, dcfiant trust. Vicky with Buddy's understandable but frustrating caution.

Cay and Wally kept talking about how God had set the whole thing up. The timing, the parallels, the struggles. Nick wasn't quite ready to buy into that, but it sure did have the look of a convincing argument.

Nick held Buddy's gaze. *C'mon. You're halfway there. Come on over here and see what kind of life is waiting for you. I promise, it won't be anything like before.*

Nick could have sworn Buddy understood. The horse tilted his head in an all-too-human *Are you sure about that?* gesture.

"No," Nick replied out loud, although he wasn't sure why. "I'm not sure about anything lately."

Dunk raised his head from where he was poking his muzzle in a hay bale, and for a second Nick worried the sudden movement would spook Buddy.

Nick turned to see Vicky standing there. He'd been so focused on connecting his gaze with Buddy he hadn't even heard her come into the barn.

"I feel like that most days," she said. "Not sure of much of anything." She walked to the edge of the pen a few feet from Nick. She was always careful to keep a sizable distance between them. "What are you and Buddy talking about?" she asked.

He was grateful she didn't find it odd he talked to horses. You had to talk to them. They responded to your voice. They were remarkable listeners. And if you knew how to listen, they talked to you, too.

Dunk came up to Vicky and said hello. Nick cocked his head in the direction of the horse still standing in the center of the pen. "Why those last twenty feet are worth it."

Vicky stroked one of Dunk's large ears. He was like a dog, that donkey—putty in your hands if you stroked his ears. "What aren't you sure of?" she asked.

Nick laughed softly. "If those last twenty feet are worth it, I suppose." Of course, he was unsure of so much more. But it wasn't his place to dive into that—not until she told him he was ready. If she ever was ready.

"That makes no sense."

"Well," Nick replied, "Not much of this makes sense. Only it's right. They should be here. They'll be okay now. I want to think they know it. Dunk does, maybe, but Buddy has a long twenty feet to go."

"Will he? Make it?"

Nick knew, by the way she phrased the question, that Buddy and Dunk were representing the same parallels in her life that they were in his. Was that good or bad? Divine Providence to be trusted, or just the tempting lie of dumb luck? He gave the only answer that applied to all of it: "I want him to." Somehow in the past fifteen days he'd become so deeply invested in these animals and this family that he truly didn't know what he'd do if it didn't all work out. This wasn't supposed to feel like his last shot at redemption, but somehow it was.

"We don't always get what we want." If bone-deep weariness and sorrow had a sound, it was the sigh Vicky let out behind those words. *Takes pain to know pain*, he thought, and then chided himself. He'd failed. That was painful, but it was nothing compared to the pain of Vicky's loss. Or Taylor's.

Something told him to keep talking. He wasn't a natural conversationalist, but the silence of the barn was too much. Nick watched the way Dunk reacted to Vicky's touch and felt a glimmer of hope. "I just don't know how hard it's gonna be for both of them to come all the way back."

"What will make the difference, you think?"

Now it was his turn to sigh. "It's never an X plus Y equals Z kind of thing. You show 'em all kinds of care, heal the wounds you can, be patient, all that stuff. But it's up to them whether or not they decide they can trust you. It's different for every animal, every situation. Can't be too different than what you do, is it?"

"Perhaps." She didn't bother to elaborate. Nick didn't like letting the silence settle between them like a hedge, but he wasn't sure what else he could do. Except whack through that hedge just a little bit and see if she peered through whatever hole he made. So, Nick chose to whack.

"Do you blame me?" There was no need to ask about what.

She did not offer a reply. Buddy, however, took a step forward. And right there was the wonder of horses—if you listened, they talked to you. Buddy was saying to keep going.

"It's okay if you do," he said. The words came thick and regretful. "*I* blame me." Every day since Roger's death, the blame followed him like a shadow.

"I want to know what happened." She said it quietly, as if her words tore the lid off a very big, very dark box of secrets. In many ways, it did.

"Did you read the reports?" He wasn't evading. He really did want to know if she'd read the official version of what happened that day. Because in his view, the official version and the real-life version, while factually the same, were very different things.

Vicky's eyes narrowed and darkened. "Every word. Dozens of times." After a pause, she added, "You were exonerated." That final word came out with a bitter edge.

So they were going to have this conversation finally. Well, maybe this was the best place to have it. And maybe Buddy and Dunk were the best witnesses to this.

"On paper, yes. I followed procedure. But if you're asking did I do the right thing? The answer is no."

"Tell me why."

It's what he'd come here to do, wasn't it? Still, it felt as if she'd asked him to hollow out his chest and leave it on the barn floor. This conversation would leave a hole in him that wouldn't ever heal. Still, he hoped that a cleansed and open wound would hurt less than the festering one.

"Are you ready to hear it?"

A determination steeled her eyes. He was looking at a strong woman. He admired her for that. Still, she handed his words back to him. "I'm not sure about anything lately."

That was as much of an invitation as he was ever to get. "Fair enough." Nick motioned to the low wall of hay bales behind them in the barn. It seemed like the kind of conversation one ought to have sitting down.

He settled himself on one hay bale, watching her perch on the edge of one a few feet over. Nick looked down at his boots and the barn floor for a moment, gathering his thoughts. He'd rehearsed this speech a million times and still found himself wildly unprepared.

"Poaching is mostly about deer, antelope, and bears out here. Rustling cattle, too. Roger and I suspected theft was expanding into horses. Nothing firm, just things we'd see here and there. And that would mean a step up from the little guys to the big crime rings. So we were watching."

Vicky relaxed a bit from her stiff stance. He gave her a moment to add anything if she wanted, but she remained silent. So he continued.

"'Course you know we got a lot of ground to cover out here. The routine stuff we do solo. Always have. It's not like we're swimming in manpower, so unless there's a good reason to call in reinforcements, we're on our own."

Those words tasted sour on Nick's tongue.

"Roger stumbled onto something. Evidence of horse theft on a bigger scale. Nothing for sure, but Roger was always of the opinion that it was coming. Not if, just a matter of when. I believed him. The higher-ups, not so much. Roger was always butting heads with them about it." He ventured a look at Vicky. "Your husband could be a stubborn man."

She gave him a look of acknowledgment and the slightest of nods. That was enough for him to keep going.

"Roger came across a small herd tucked away in a remote location. Not exactly a hideout, but definitely an operation. Young kids, it looked like. Youth tends to mean bold and stupid. Usually, it's because they convinced themselves they've come up with some new way to outwit us that we haven't seen before. Only in this case, it was true."

"Meaning what?"

"Meaning it was a much bigger operation than it looked like. Only we didn't know that until…" Nick didn't finish that sentence.

She finished it for him. "Until they shot him."

"And I wasn't there. I should have been, and I wasn't." Nick had always wondered how much it would hurt to say those words to her face.

Now he knew.

It hurt beyond his worst imagination.

Chapter Nine

"I should have been there, and I wasn't."

Vicky waited for some satisfaction to hit her. All the paperwork, the inquiries about procedure and evidence and such, had insisted the situation did not warrant a call for backup. The phrases that had been used were "expected to operate independently" and "call for backup only in high-risk situations" and "large-scale theft."

None of that changed the bone-deep pain that Roger had been alone and outgunned when he died. The fact that it was a total surprise did not change the outcome. He should have been able to call for backup on a hunch. She'd carried that sour weight every day since the officers came to her home and delivered the news that had dropped her to her knees.

It felt like she'd been crawling through life on her hands and knees ever since.

Now, hearing the pain and massive regret in Nick's voice, Vicky realized Nick had been doing the same thing. While buckling under a different version of the burden she bore.

Maybe it really was time to stop. Or to try stopping. To cross her own version of Buddy's twenty feet. It might be worth it. It certainly couldn't be worse.

Vicky decided to ask the question that hounded her this

whole time. "Did he ask you to come with him?" She'd always assumed that Roger had asked Nick to back him up and Nick declined, opting to follow procedure. They were friends—partners, really, although the wildlife service didn't really have formal partners like police officers did. Of course Roger would ask for backup if he thought he needed it.

Wouldn't he? Vicky realized she was afraid of the answer to that question. It could change a lot of things.

Nick paused for a long moment before answering. Surely he recognized how much hinged on his answer. "Yes and no."

She'd come this far, she wasn't going to let Nick get off with an answer like that. "What do you mean?" Out of the corner of her eye she saw Dunk's ears twitch at the sharp tone of her reply.

Nick rubbed his hands on his knees, still hunched over and looking at the barn floor. She recognized the stiff posture of someone reaching back into a painful memory—mostly because she did it so often.

"We'd been talking on the phone the day before. He told me he was going to check on a hunch down in a more remote location. Roger always had crazy good hunches—it was almost spooky how he could put tiny details together. It's what made him so good at what he did."

That wasn't the answer she was looking for, but Nick was leading up to the moment so she let him continue.

"He got me on the radio—cell service was rotten that far out—and said he was onto something. 'Looks wrong. Too simple,' he'd said. A small-looking operation to distract from a larger one. 'So I'm going to poke the bear and see what happens,' he said."

That sounded like Roger. He was always going to try

something and "see what happens." There were times when that attitude brought amazing surprises. And times when he poked the bear and got scratched.

"So no, he didn't come straight out and ask for backup," Nick went on. "It'd be asking me to break with procedure, to leave my assignment and back him up on his. It also would have taken me about two hours to get where he was. And you know how much patience that man had."

Roger was a wonderful man, but he could be as impatient as he was impulsive. Roses just because it was Wednesday was lovely. Buying a bigger truck without discussing it with her just because it seemed a great deal, not so much.

Nick finally looked up at her. "But I could have. I heard it in his voice. I heard the question he didn't actually ask. I knew how good his instincts were. I could have maybe just talked him into waiting the two hours it would take me to get there. Or to go ask the supervisor to okay it. But I didn't. I didn't do any of that."

The pain in his voice and his eyes seemed to go straight through her. She saw in him what she'd always known: the fact that Nick had technically done nothing wrong, that he'd technically followed correct procedure, meant next to nothing.

Nick stood up and walked a ways away as if he couldn't stand making the admission near to her. "He was protecting *me*." His voice filled the empty space of the barn. "When I should have been protecting him. Keeping him safe for you and Taylor. What good is a mountain of policies and procedures if you don't follow them? And look at what it cost you."

Even though Vicky was sitting on a bale of hay, something seemed to slip out from under her feet. The assumption Nick had refused to help Roger had become a familiar pain, a comfortable—maybe even righteous—anger. She couldn't hold tight to that anymore, and it left her feeling adrift and off-balance.

"I was always so sure he asked you. And that you'd said no."

Nick turned back toward her, still staying a distance away. "He never outright asked me, but I think he was counting on me to show up anyway. Some part of me knew that, and I ignored it. Everything would have been different if I hadn't. It's not an excuse, but I'd gotten written up for not following some stupid procedure a month earlier, and it made me think twice about going."

He leaned up against the pen fence as if the weight of his admission pressed him against the planks. "The one time ignoring procedure would have been the right thing, and I failed. Failed him and you. I had nothing to lose and Roger had everything to lose. What's more cowardly than that?"

Vicky had heard the phrase "painful truth" hundreds of times. She'd used it when counseling pet owners about illness or suffering in their beloved animals. The truth she heard now was so much more than that. It shook everything. She looked down at her hands, not especially surprised to see they'd tightened into fists. Now she was going to have to open those fists, only she didn't know how.

"That's why you disappeared."

"Stayed away" was too tame a term. Nick had vanished from her life and Taylor's. It had left a void so large she'd filled it with anger and blame.

"I thought I could run from it. After all, as far as the Wildlife Service was concerned I did nothing wrong. I asked for a reassignment as far from here as I could manage. Turns out I could have been the other side of the world and it wouldn't have made a difference."

"Why did you come back? Why now?" Vicky surprised herself by really wanting to know.

"When I fell and hurt my knee, the best orthopedic surgeon I could find was in Spokane. I figured the other side of the state was far enough away from here. I stumbled across Buddy and Dunk near Bozeman and… I don't know, I just felt like I couldn't stand another round of ignoring someone I could help. And when I heard your mom and aunts had started this rescue farm—" he waved his hand around the barn "—it all made sense."

The insistence of Mom and the aunts that Nick, Dunk, and Buddy had not come here by chance rang too true. What were the odds of all those details lining up except by God's hand? God's unrelenting pursuit of her deliverance from this long road of pain?

But what would there be for her when the pain was gone?

Vicky's answer didn't come from wisdom or prayer or divine revelation. It came from Buddy.

Buddy, without either Nick or her realizing it, had crossed the last twenty feet to their edge of the pen. In fact, Buddy had walked right up to Nick and stood next to him.

Dunk walked over to Buddy and put his head on the horse's flank as if to say, "Welcome back, friend."

What would come in place of the void? Vicky knew now. It would be healing. For her, for her son, for everyone in this barn. Not quick, nor easy, but healing all the same.

After such an enormous moment, Nick couldn't quite figure out what to say to Vicky now. He ought to feel some sense of completion, of having done what he'd come to do.

Only he didn't. He felt incomplete and uncomfortable. As if they'd come Buddy's twenty feet, only to discover they had a hundred feet more to go.

As Vicky turned to go, he realized the one thing that had not been said in this conversation. "I'm sorry. More than I'll probably ever be able to tell you. Or Taylor."

She met his gaze. And the edge of anger and blame wasn't there with its usual force. Now it was just a shadow cast over her eyes. One he recognized. It had probably been over his own eyes for so long he almost didn't even notice it anymore. Regret.

"You have told me." She stated it like a simple fact. After all, they both knew he could be sorry with every inch of his being and it wouldn't change anything.

Out of nowhere, Nick felt an odd, out-of-place smile find its way to the corners of his mouth. "Probably have to do it a lot more."

Vicky offered him the first smile he'd seen from her since his arrival. "I suppose you will."

And there it was. The moment he'd really come for: the point where he and Vicky chose to find their way out of this valley, agreed to find a way to heal. He'd thought it would be a solo job—him convincing her, striving to earn her forgiveness. Instead, they were like Buddy and Dunk. The most unlikely of teams, each helping the other.

Taylor's voice came calling from the direction of the big house, and Vicky turned to go. Somehow the barn seemed lighter, larger, and yet closer at the same time. The word *holy* popped into his mind, completely shocking him. As if all Cay's insistence that this had been orchestrated *for* him, not *by* him, could be true.

Nick watched her leave the barn, wondering if the way the sunshine glowed around her was just his imagination. She seemed to walk with a lighter step. He felt lighter. Fragile, scared, but lighter.

The scared part came from the realization he *did* want

more. He'd come the proverbial twenty feet of telling her why he'd done what he'd done the day Roger died. Did he deserve to be part of Vicky's and Taylor's lives? Did he have any right to his affection for Taylor? And what on earth was he supposed to do about the baffling pull he was starting to feel toward Vicky?

Nick walked back over to the hay bales and slumped down on one, stunned by what he'd just admitted to himself. He wanted more than forgiveness from Vicky? Was there anything more impossible—maybe even outright wrong—than that?

He was so lost in the tangle of these thoughts that Nick wasn't sure how much time had passed when he heard a deep voice from the barn door. "You okay in here?"

"Uh…yeah," he muttered, pretty sure he sounded anything but okay.

An impressively tall man walked into the barn, and Nick recognized him as Grant Emerson. He was Cay's son and Meg from the diner's husband. They lived in the smaller house on the other side of the property.

"My cousin Vicky looked a little shell-shocked when she left just now. I know you two have…history. You say something to upset her?"

If he didn't already know Grant was part of High Mountain's police force, it would have been easy to see the law enforcement background in the guy. He was direct and protective.

Nick wasn't sure how much of the earth-shifting conversation he'd had with Vicky he ought to convey. So he shrugged. "Sort of cleared the air a bit, I think."

Grant walked closer, leaning back up against the pen fence much the way Nick had done earlier. The man was so large he nearly dwarfed Dunk and stood eye to eye with

Buddy. "She likes everyone to think she's doing fine. I don't think she is. I wouldn't take well to you making things harder for her."

Right there was another reason why his presence in Vicky's and Taylor's life was a very dicey prospect indeed. "Believe it or not, I think things just got a little bit easier."

"Mind explaining that?"

Nick almost had to laugh. "Not sure I can."

Grant's dark gaze said *"Try."*

Nick drew his hands down his face, groping for how to talk about it. "I know she blames me. I blame me. But we had to get to the place where we could talk about what happened. About why. It seemed like the only way to get unstuck."

"It's why you came here." Grant cocked his head toward Buddy and Dunk. "Why you brought them here. So you could tell her your side of the story."

If there was one thing the past hour had shown Nick, it was that there weren't really sides to this. Just parts hidden and parts revealed. Much as it might make things easier, there was no black and white—only a dozen shades of gray. "At first," seemed the only honest answer. "Only I knew we couldn't talk about it until she asked. Until she was ready."

"And today was that day?"

"Seems so."

Grant put one hand in his pocket. "Now what?" Was the guy being intentionally intimidating, or was that just his personality?

The truth seemed like the best option. "No idea."

"I suppose I should appreciate your honesty," Grant said.

"I don't want to mess this up. We got over a big hurdle today, but we have a long way to go."

Grant surprised him by walking over and taking a seat

on the hay bale Vicky had been sitting on. "You plan on being around a while?"

Nick stretched out his bad leg, suddenly reminded of how stiff and sore it felt. "I got four weeks of medical leave to go. At first I didn't know how much of it I'd spend here."

"And now?"

"I guess I'd like to see how far I can get patching things up here. Maybe be the godfather to Taylor I was supposed to be." Nick felt compelled to add, "Before..."

"Big difference between before and after in this case. It'll take a lot of work. It's Vicky's call, of course, but my mother seems to think you deserve a second chance." Grant swept a hand around the barn. "The aunts are big on second chances."

Nick wasn't sure what to make of that statement. "Good cause," he said, stumped for a better reply.

"Are you a good cause?" Grant asked. The words were a challenge, but his tone held no judgment. "I know what other people say, but I want to know what you say."

Grant was giving Nick the same open door Vicky had just given him. Nick recognized the moment for what it was. "I hope to be. I want to be. Your cousin deserves to stop carrying around all that pain and anger. And I think we're both tired of all the regret." High-sounding words, but it was truly how he felt. Then he nodded toward Buddy and Dunk, who still hadn't moved from their new places, watching them from the fence. "I don't know what healing looks like, but heading in that direction seems like a good cause to me."

Grant thought about that for a moment and actually turned his gaze to the horse and donkey as if they'd offered up an opinion. "Long shot, long haul," he said.

"Seems to me most good causes are," Nick replied.

For whatever reason, that answer seemed to satisfy Grant, and he stood. "Don't you add to her hurt. Vicky calls the shots on this, understood?"

Nick simply nodded.

For the second time in as many hours, Nick found himself alone again in the barn, save one horse and one donkey, trying to work out how the world had just changed.

Grant was right—Vicky did need to be the one calling the shots on where they went from here. But Nick felt an odd comfort in the hope that maybe God was truly calling the shots as well.

Chapter Ten

Even on the most trying days, bedtime with Taylor was always a balm to Vicky's spirit. His drowsy eyes called to mind the days she could get lost in Roger's gaze, and the world pared down to just mother and son. Some days, just before he drifted off to sleep, her time with Taylor felt full and comforting.

It also brought out some of his most startling questions.

"Why isn't grass blue like the sky?"

"Do cows laugh?"

"Why are elbows so tickly?"

Their end-of-the-day conversations would almost always end with Vicky smiling as she watched Taylor fall asleep.

Tonight, Taylor's question pulled the rug out from underneath her. He looked her straight in the eye Monday night and said with a heartbreaking curiosity, "Why did somebody hurt Buddy and Dunk?"

Oh, Lord, please help me. How to answer that? Taylor could plainly see Buddy and Dunk had been injured. The conversations about neglect had been careful around Taylor, but they still happened. The last thing Vicky wanted was for Taylor's last thought of the day to be on such a subject.

She opted for her favorite stalling tactic when Taylor hit her with such a whopping question. "Why do you ask?"

"Buddy is such a nice horse. Why would anybody want to make him sad?"

Vicky brushed a lock of hair off Taylor's face. "I think some people don't understand that animals have feelings just like we do. They don't think about taking care of them."

His face scrunched up in thought. That wasn't enough of an answer for him.

"You know your class rabbit?" she asked. "The one you got from Three Sisters Farm?"

Taylor's face brightened. "Wiggles He's great. He's spending the summer at Jacob's house."

"Your teacher and Ms. Carly taught you and Jacob and everybody how to know when Wiggles is happy, right?"

Taylor nodded. "He jumps and his ears do things."

"So you and your class make sure Wiggles gets what he needs and you show him how much you love him. You all know that's an important part of having an animal."

"I got to fill his water bottle the last day of school. Before Jacob got to take Wiggles home."

"Exactly," Vicky went on. "Everyone knew what Wiggles needed, and no one would think to leave him alone at the school all summer because he needs food and water."

"And pets," Taylor added. "He likes getting petted between his ears."

Vicky chose her words carefully. "Sometimes, people don't think about those things. They only think about getting the animal, or having them around, but not about what it means to really take care of them." It seemed the kindest way to describe the sort of neglect Buddy and Dunk had seen. She wasn't about to broach the subject of deliberate animal abuse or poaching.

Taylor furrowed his little brow. "Well, that's just wrong."

"You're right. So when bad things happen like that, it's

important to watch for the good people to help, and to be a help ourselves when we can." She smiled at her son. "It's true of people, too. Like when we brought ice cream to Sadie when she got her tonsils out."

"I got three helper stars in school the last month," Taylor boasted.

Vicky felt her smile widen. "You most certainly did. I'm proud of what a good helper you are."

"The Horsey Man is an extra-good helper, isn't he?"

Vicky tried not to let her reaction to the sudden turn of conversation show. "Buddy and Dunk certainly are blessed to have him, that's for sure."

"He's nice. I like my boots lots."

It was still no small feat to get Taylor to choose other shoes some days. "I know you do." She forced herself to add, "That was a very nice thing for Mr. Nick to do." She was wary of the gesture at first, thinking Nick was trying to buy Taylor's affections, but she'd come to realize it had been a genuine gift.

"Is he a dad? Does he have a little boy like me at home somewhere?"

If there was one thing Vicky could be certain of, it was how alone Nick Youngston was. In many ways he was as abandoned as Dunk and Buddy—and the poignancy of that wasn't lost on her. "No," she replied gently. "He doesn't have any family."

"So no one takes care of him?"

This was venturing into challenging territory. "It's different with grown-ups. We can take care of ourselves in lots of ways."

"So why is he so sad?"

Children see so much more than we realize, Vicky thought. "Mr. Nick has had some hard things happen in his life." Perhaps this was the time to broach a topic she'd been fearing. "Did you know Mr. Nick was a ranger like Daddy was?"

"He told me they were friends. He told me Dad was special. And that he was sorry Dad went to heaven. Is that why he's sad?"

Vicky searched for a good answer to that very complicated question. "Lots of people are sad Daddy went to heaven."

"You are," Taylor said with heart-wrenching simplicity.

"Yes, I am."

"Granny says we should let him help us, even though it's funny-feeling."

So even her mother was coming around in her opinion of Nick? Taylor's term confused her, until she asked, "Funny-feeling?"

"Uncom…untable…" Taylor couldn't quite get the word out.

"Uncomfortable?"

"That one. Un-com-fit-a-ble. Funny-feeling."

There was truth in that. Especially after their last conversation, Vicky found herself awash in dozens of different, uncomfortable feelings about Nick.

"It doesn't feel funny to me, though," Taylor went on. "I like the Horsey Man."

One of the uncomfortable feelings for Vicky was exactly that—how Taylor and Nick connected. It was uncanny, really, and she didn't know what to do with that. "He's nice," she offered, ashamed she couldn't be more generous after all the man had done for Taylor and the farm.

"But he's sad. So, if I'm a good helper, I should help him. Right?"

She knew, on some level, that Taylor did have the capacity to help Nick. The redemption and forgiveness he needed was something Taylor easily granted. It was her own troubled spirit that still held on to the bitterness. She'd lived with it all of Taylor's life so that it was comfortable. But that hadn't been based on truth. She knew that now. Rearranging her life around that new truth was going to be just as her mother described: uncomfortable.

"Is that what you want to do? Help him?" she asked.

Taylor didn't have to think about it. "Yep."

"How?" She was curious how her kindhearted son would answer the question.

"Dunno. But I'll figure it out." He seemed so sure.

Vicky tried an idea that came to her. "Maybe we could start by calling him Mr. Nick instead of the Horsey Man."

Taylor scowled. "Nah. He's the Horsey Man. You can call him Mr. Nick if you want."

Vicky wondered what Nick might think about that. He seemed happy and grateful to have even the tiniest part in her and Taylor's life. Where did it go from here? Vicky expected Nick was just as unsure as she was.

One thing could not be denied. Since their talk two days ago in the barn, finally taking the step to discuss the thing that weighed so heavily on both their hearts, the weight had lifted a bit. Nick Youngston wasn't the enemy anymore. Perhaps he was just a fellow traveler on the path to healing.

"Like Buddy and Dunk," Taylor was saying. He'd continued talking as she was lost in her thoughts.

They were all too much like Buddy and Dunk, weren't they? Each helping the other move past their wounds to see what lay beyond them. The notion was so eerily accurate—and unsettling—that Vicky almost shivered.

"We'll help him. Like Buddy and Dunk help him," Taylor went on. “He told me they help him as much as he helps them. So everybody’s better.”

Vicky kissed her son’s forehead. “Sounds good to me. You get some sleep now, you hear? So you can be a great helper again tomorrow.”

She switched on the night-light, pulled the chain to turn off Taylor’s nightstand lamp, and gave a soft thanks for the wonder of her son and the way he saw the world.

Chapter Eleven

Wednesday evening, Aunt Cay's massive porch was packed with people. Nearly the whole McNally family—everyone who was in town, plus spouses—were gathered in chairs and benches to plan the First Annual High Mountain Pet Parade. Even Vicky's brother Zack was on hand. That was notable, because Zack was often too busy with his own large ranch nearby to show up for these things.

"Well, what do you think?" Vicky's mother asked. She'd just laid out a rather impressive plan for the event.

Aunt Peggy had a smile as wide as the porch. "It's wonderful! I love everything about it."

Vicky could have predicted the responses. Grant was trying to hide his frown, convinced—as he often was—that the three sisters had bitten off more than they could chew. Meg seemed charmed by the whole idea. Her daughters would love parading some of the farm's dogs through the town. Cay was, of course, enthusiastic, because Cay was enthusiastic about everything.

She suddenly noticed everyone was looking at her. Most notably, Zack was keenly focused on her. There were nearly half a dozen people on this porch—why were everyone's eyes fixed on her?

Nick. It had been the arrival of Buddy and Dunk that

spurred the idea for the parade to help cover the large expenses for taking the animals on.

This wasn't about Nick. At least, it shouldn't be about Nick. The growing role he was taking in her life pricked at her. Details were lining up in significant ways that were getting harder to ignore. He was here for a reason beyond Buddy and Dunk.

She'd always known that, of course. It was just sinking deeper—especially after that last conversation in the barn. For a woman who'd been waiting a long time for things to get better, the change in front of her didn't feel better. It just felt very different. And very hard.

"What do you think, V?" Her brother had always called her V, and it was a comfort to hear him use the nickname. Zack was just a busy rancher, but his distance since Roger's death stung because it felt like another abandonment. She knew that wasn't true, but not much in the way she felt about the world lately followed logic.

"It's a good idea," she replied. "But there are some things we should pay attention to. With all those animals in one place, if one or two get out of control, it might be hard to manage."

"You're talking about the horse and the donkey," Zack said. "You think we shouldn't include them."

"We can't not include them," Aunt Cay cried out. "It's all about them."

Zack frowned. "We're not talking about someone's cute puppy, Aunt Cay. That's a large horse. It hasn't even been a month. No one should be putting Taylor up on that horse."

"No one's talking about doing that. Besides, Taylor wants to ride Dunk." Vicky was surprised to find herself getting defensive about the idea. "Nick promised me that if he feels Dunk is in any way—in *any* way—unsafe for Taylor to ride, that it won't happen."

"The little guy's got his heart set on it," Cay said. "No one wants to disappoint him, least of all Nick."

"And we're going on his word, are we?" It was quite clear what Zack thought of Nick's opinion.

"Well, you've certainly got a hefty opinion for someone who hasn't clocked a lot of time on this farm," Mom shot back. She was the only one who got away with talking to Zack like that. And her mother was probably the only one her brother held his tongue for when he got like this.

"Nick has a lot of experience with this sort of thing," Cay replied. "He has some reservations about Buddy, but he believes Dunk will be ready for the parade. And you'd be amazed at the progress he's made with Buddy. The man has a gift, I tell you." Cay gave just the briefest of looks in Vicky's direction before adding, "I'm glad he's here. We've changed those animals' lives, and that's the whole reason we're doing this."

Mom shifted topics. "And we can't do it well without more funds. I've kept the parade entry fee small, and there will be booths along the parade route where you can vote for your favorite for a five-dollar donation."

"Votes?" Grant questioned. "We're going to turn this into a popularity contest?"

"For the most creative costumes," Cay replied. "Honestly, Grant, no one's pitting cats against dogs or gerbils against bunnies."

"No, we're just going to condemn High Mountain's animal population to dressing up in who knows what."

Meg gave her husband a teasing smile. "Lots of people like dressing up their pets. Have you seen Pastor Jim's dachshund? He wears a different sweater every week." Meg looked at Cay. "Honestly, was this man ever fun?"

In fact, Grant had lightened up considerably since marrying Meg. She was working wonders on Grant's formerly grumpy—well, grumpier—demeanor.

"What about sponsors, Meg?" Aunt Peggy asked before Cay could say anything about her son. "How's that going?"

"Well," Meg replied. "There are four corners on the parade route, so we're looking for four High Mountain businesses to be sponsors and get signs put up for their donation. I've got the bank and the grocery store so far, so we only need two more. Wally at the store has agreed to make sponsor signs."

"And we're still set to use the church lawn as the spot where everyone ends up." Mom confirmed. "A party with cookies and lemonade and all."

"Except for Nick, Buddy, and Dunk," Vicky added. They'd talked about how it was best if those two animals went back to the farm in the trailer after the parade. "Nick will bring them back here."

"Are you sure they can't stay?" Peggy protested. "They are sort of our animal grand marshals, after all. How can the three of them miss the party?"

"Both Nick and I feel the parade and the party might be too much for them." Vicky was fully prepared to not have them appear at all if their progress didn't give her or Nick the confidence they could handle it. That would surely disappoint Taylor, but his and everyone's safety needed to come first.

"Glad to see he's taking your welfare into account," Zack said without any real gladness in his voice.

"We're taking *everyone's* welfare into account," Vicky

retorted. "Buddy is a large horse. Even if Dunk does perfectly, it's not smart to separate them."

They wrapped up a bunch of other details over the next half an hour. It was a classic McNally sisters operation—an overdose of joy, mixed with a splash of happy chaos, wrapped up in their trademark optimism. No matter what her mother and aunts took on, it always seemed to work out well in the end. Perhaps that's what made it so hard to feel unhealed the way she did. She should have their resilience in her blood, but it didn't seem to work that way.

Zack caught her as she left the kitchen after leaving some flea and tick medication for the dogs with Cay.

"You're taking his side now?" There was no need to elaborate who and what he meant.

"I'm not taking sides on anything."

"You're the vet. But you're listening to his advice? After everything that's happened?"

It was hard enough to view Nick in even a slightly positive light without Zack pushing back against it. Vicky took a deep breath. Her big brother was being protective. He was being a bit hard-nosed about it, but she tried to view it as coming from a place of love.

"I am not an equine vet. I'm not even a large animal vet. And this isn't standard care, this is rehabilitation from neglect. He knows way more about this than I do, and I'm not so bitter that I can't accept his advice."

Zack raised an eyebrow, and Vicky regretted that the word *bitter* had slipped out.

"Grant told me he gave Nick a warning. To be honest, I would have if he hadn't."

Vicky wanted to grind her teeth. Grant had already walked back across the field to the house where he lived with Meg, and she considered going after him and telling him what she thought of that. She settled for an annoyed, "How like him. You all can stop worrying about me. I'm fine. I can handle myself."

"You aren't fine and you know it," Zack shot back. "He shouldn't be here. Not after what he did to you. He can't just wipe that away with a pony ride."

That went too far. "Stop it, Zack. I admit this isn't very comfortable at the moment, but it's my situation to work through. We've actually started to talk about it. I'm learning more about what happened."

Zack swept a hand toward the barn. "So you're just going to forgive him? For leaving Roger to walk into that alone?"

"No." The word was immediate, dark, and surged up with force from somewhere inside. "But I'm trying to understand. That's not the same thing."

"Will you forgive him?"

That was the real question here. Could she forgive Nick, even when she knew all the facts? There was still a mountain of resentment and years of blame, holed up inside her. Part of her recognized the facts Nick had shared, but they didn't seem to counter all the emotions she still carried.

"I don't know."

Maybe she couldn't just yet.

Nick rolled his shoulders and wiped his forehead on Friday afternoon. He had forgotten how hot it could get up here in the mountains. Especially with a dozen yards of fencing to set up stretching in front of him.

Still, the work felt good. It made his knee ache something fierce, but it was a well-used ache instead of the stagnant ache that chased him in the early days of limited activity. It was fine with him if being useful hurt.

Wally had helped him for several days, but today the

man needed to be at the feed store. Nick didn't mind being on his own this afternoon. He welcomed the wide-open space to sort through his thoughts. They were a tangle after last weekend's conversation with Vicky. They'd talked about what happened. Sure, it was hard and painful, but it was a start. A small step in the right direction.

What surprised him most was how much he was craving spending time with Taylor. The little guy looked at him with no reservations, none of the dark edge he got from most of the people in town. He'd expected that. Steeled himself for it, actually. It was just that Taylor's complete lack of judgment stood out like a beacon, calling to him.

"Horsey man!"

As if summoned by his thoughts, Nick looked up to see Vicky's truck speeding across the field with Taylor in the cab seat behind her. He immediately caught the frantic look in their eyes. Dropping the pair of pliers he'd been holding, Nick started off at full speed toward the truck.

"It's Buddy," Vicky said when she pulled close enough. "Peggy was letting the dogs out for a run and one of them got into the pen somehow. It set Buddy off."

Nick launched himself into the bed of the truck without a moment's thought, ignoring the massive shot of pain from his knee. "Go, go!" he called as he made his way to the front of the truck bed where the open window let him talk to Vicky. From his booster seat closer to the back window, Taylor looked frightened.

"It's okay, sport. Buddy's just got a fright." It wasn't normal for a horse to have this strong a reaction to the presence of a dog, but this wasn't a normal situation. Nick hoped it wouldn't be a major setback. Still, he wasn't about to speculate in front of Taylor.

"Was there anyone in there with him? Anyone in there now?" Nick tried to keep the alarm from his voice.

"No. Cay managed to call the dog back out of the pen, but Buddy is still..." He could see her face in the rearview mirror, searching for the most calming word to use in front of Taylor. "Upset."

It didn't quite work. "I'm scared for Buddy, Mommy. Oscar is a good doggy. Buddy's gonna be okay, right?"

The boy's frightened tone twisted inside Nick's chest. "Don't worry, Taylor. I know just how to calm Buddy down." He tried another affirmation. "Just like your mom knows what to do when you're scared."

"We sing and hold hands," Taylor offered. Nick wished he could see the boy's face, but the rearview mirror only showed Vicky's. "But Mommy's hands are driving."

It wasn't even a decision. Nick reached through the truck cab's back window and offered his hand to Taylor. "Then I guess mine'll just have to do."

Realizing he should have gotten some kind of okay from Vicky first, Nick glanced at her reflection with an eyebrow raised. She looked startled, but then gave a slight nod just as Nick felt Taylor's small hand in his.

He knew in that moment, despite the bumpy ride and worrisome circumstances, that he would never forget the feeling of Taylor's hand. The softness of his little fingers as they gripped his palm, how small and fragile they felt in his rough, calloused hands.

"It's gonna be fine, Taylor," he said as he gave the boy's hand a return squeeze. "Don't worry. What do we sing?"

"Anything," Taylor replied. Already his voice lost a bit of its earlier tension.

"You are my sunshine," Vicky began in a soft, uncertain voice. Full of a mother's tenderness. Nick found it one of the most beautiful things he'd ever heard. Another piece of the hard shell around him cracked open.

Taylor joined in, and the shell cracked further. The bumps in the field jolted the truck, but the song kept on.

"You gotta sing, too," Taylor insisted.

It felt beyond foolish, but also somehow the right thing to do. Even though he knew he possessed nothing close to a singing voice, Nick joined in. Off-key, but with as much reassurance as he could manage. Taylor kept his hand tight in Nick's until they pulled up to the barn.

Vicky's face was a mixture of emotions as she climbed out of the cab while Nick vaulted himself out of the bed. Worry, wonder, gratitude, and something else he saw that likely matched the riot going off in his own chest. "Gimme a minute," he called to her, even as she heard Taylor undoing the buckles of his booster seat.

"You don't sing too good," Taylor said with an innocent smile.

Nick could almost laugh. "Don't I know it. But hey, you asked."

Cay and Peggy were outside the barn, looking worried. He could hear barking from the dog pen off the barn—that probably wasn't helping things. From inside the barn, he heard anxious sounds from both Buddy and Dunk. How they got through the next twenty minutes was going to tell him a lot about how progress would go from here.

Now, Lord? He found himself asking God. *This is the worst time for this to happen.* Still, Nick also found himself sending up a small prayer of thanks for the precious moment in the truck. Maybe that's how God worked—little gems nestled inside big troubles.

He stopped in front of Cay. "Can you take the dogs

somewhere where Buddy and Dunk can't hear them? The other side of the house or something?"

"I'll get the leashes and take them out back," Peggy said.

"Good. Nobody goes inside until I say, got it?"

Peggy and Cay nodded.

Vicky and Taylor had come up by then, so Nick caught Taylor's wary gaze. "Let me go in and talk to them first, okay? You can come in soon, but not yet."

Nick turned back toward the barn. He stood still, closing his eyes, and forcing calm into his body. The feeling of Taylor's small hand in his came back to him in a strong flood, and he pulled in a deep breath with the memory. He couldn't mirror the animal's fright; they'd sense it immediately. He had to walk into that barn as a source of calm.

When he felt his pulse lower enough, he walked inside.

Buddy's eyes were wide. His nostrils were flared. Dunk was even more noisy than usual, as if calling out for someone to help his friend. Both animals were darting around the pen as if looking for a way to escape. He'd seen it happen before. Maybe Dunk wasn't strong enough to knock down the pen fence, but in this state, Buddy very well could manage a breakout. In that case, all might be lost.

Fortunately, they'd managed to get a halter on Buddy yesterday. That made things easier. Nick walked up to the spot on the wall where all the tack hung, thankful that he and Wally had made sure the sisters had all the equipment they needed. If he could snap on a long lead, Nick could slowly direct Buddy into a controlled circle. Horses processed things by walking. Worked for people, too, for that matter. They all had a lot to process at the moment.

"Okay, Buddy. I know you got a fright, but it's okay." He kept his voice calm and steady. "Hey, Dunk, you want to help us all out a bit by taking it down a notch?"

From out behind him in the barn, Nick heard four voices singing. He smiled, imagining the quartet holding hands. He knew a lot of rehab tactics, but there was still nothing that worked better than outright love. With that, surely they could get over this hurdle.

He stood by the edge of the pen, lead in hand. Buddy was still moving wildly, but Dunk worked his way over to Nick in a collection of loops and zigzags. Finally the donkey's braying ceased, and he angled his fuzzy gray head toward Nick.

"Thanks, dude," he said to Dunk's big eyes. "I really need your help on this one."

He held a short conversation with the donkey, not really paying attention to the words but just sounding as calm as possible. As he talked, he moved closer to Buddy, who still paced back and forth like a lion at the zoo. Nick made sure to say both animals' names in soothing voices.

This was no time to be brave or bold. Nick had known the pain of a horse's kick, bite, and how many weeks it took his toes to heal when a horse had stamped on his foot. Horses were powerful animals, but they were still prey animals. Threat sent them into behavior that often couldn't be controlled. It was why trust was such a crucial component of rehabilitation—and why it was so damaging for a horse to lose it.

After more time than he would have liked, Nick got close enough to Buddy to snap on the lead. "There you go. There you go," he kept repeating, keeping the lead slack and following Buddy's arcs as he walked. "Look at Dunk here. He's over it. Let's you and I do the same."

Chapter Twelve

"It's taking a long time, Mommy," Taylor whined.

"I know." Vicky found all her professional calm had left her. Clinically, she knew what was likely happening in there. Calming an anxious animal was never a predictable process. She'd been called to the animal shelter in the neighboring town enough times to know a setback like this for an abused animal could take weeks to overcome. Still, she had faith in Nick's uncanny abilities with Buddy. She also had faith in Dunk's resilience and companionship.

"Maybe we should go inside and let Mr. Nick do what he needs to do," Cay offered.

"Nope," Taylor said immediately. "I wanna stay here. I'll wait."

"It could take a long time, honey," Vicky advised.

As if to declare his intention, Taylor plunked himself down on the grass under the nearby tree.

"Well, then, I guess we're staying here." Peggy eased herself down on the grass beside Taylor.

"If that's so, I'm going inside to get some lemonade," Cay announced. "It's a hot one today."

"And some cookies?" Taylor suggested eagerly.

"And some cookies, *please*," Vicky corrected.

Taylor complied, and Cay answered, "I think that's a fine idea. Be back in a jiffy."

After a moment, Taylor began playing with some sticks he found by the tree's thick trunk. Vicky was struck by the instant and total confidence Taylor had in Nick's abilities. That could mean her son didn't fully understand the seriousness of what was happening in the barn. It could also mean he just knew the Horsey Man would take care of it.

Trusting Nick. Was she capable of such a thing after three years of resenting him? Blaming him? Her head knew some of that resentment and anger had been misplaced. But, as Pastor Jim was so fond of saying, sometimes it could be a long distance from the head to the heart. The most surprising thing had taken place as they barreled the truck across the field, catching a glimpse of Taylor's hand in Nick's, hearing the man's almost comically off-key voice singing with her son.

She *wanted* to trust him. Nick was turning out to be someone so different than the man she'd built up in her thoughts. He was quiet and humble, physically imposing but just as ready to hunch down and connect with Taylor. She'd been so suspicious of his motives, only to discover they seemed genuine.

Peggy's voice pulled her from her thoughts. "I'm thankful we have Nick. I didn't know what to do when things got so wild in there. I know Buddy doesn't have all his strength back yet, but he's still a big animal, and strong."

Vicky didn't reply. Mostly because her own thoughts on the subject of Nick Youngston were in a chaotic state as well. "You've taken on a big project with those two." She noticed that things had quieted down in the barn and hoped that was a good sign.

"I suppose. But there's just something about those two.

They belong here." Peggy's gaze shifted to the barn. "All three of us agreed from the moment Nick brought them to us, even though we don't know much about what we're doing. Then again, that's how it's always turned out with whatever animal God sends us."

Vicky gave a laugh. "This is a bit of a leap from bunnies and puppies."

"True, but there wouldn't be a lot of faith required for us to stick with just the little cute critters. This one's a big leap of trust." After a pause, Peggy added, "For everyone. After all, there's a leap of faith and trust in this for you, too."

"True."

"How are you feeling about all this?" Peggy checked to see that Taylor's attention was elsewhere before lowering her voice. "Your mother told me what Nick told you. That Roger's death, terrible as it was, wasn't all on Nick the way we've all thought. How are you feeling about that?"

Vicky put her hand on her chest. "To be honest, there's a whole lot of Dunk's stubbornness bumping around in here."

Peggy laughed. "Well, no one can fault you for that. But it seems to me that part of Dunk's charm is how open his little donkey heart is. Ready to think the world that hurt him before might just be a nice place to call home now. I think that's why I like the little guy so much."

"Maybe I'm more like Buddy, then."

Peggy gave a little *hmm.* "I'm coming to think there's a bit of Buddy and a bit of Dunk in all of us. We all need each other because they need each other."

Vicky raised a skeptical eyebrow at her aunt's dose of equine wisdom. "They've still got a long way to go, Aunt Peggy."

Peggy smiled. "Don't we all, hon. Don't we all."

Cay arrived with an impromptu picnic, as if the whole

thing were an adventure rather than a barely averted crisis. "I brought an extra glass for Nick. I expect he's working hard in there and could use a cool drink."

They munched on cookies and drank lemonade while they waited for Nick to give an all clear. Taylor was getting antsy despite the snacks, and Vicky wondered if they'd truly be able to wait and see the outcome.

In another twenty minutes, Nick appeared out of the barn door. He looked strained, but there was a glint of victory in his eyes. Taylor practically knocked over his lemonade in a rush to get to Nick, but Vicky snagged his hand. "Hang on there. Let Mr. Nick come over here and tell us what's happened."

Sweat darkened his T-shirt and shone on his arms. "We're over the worst of it," he pronounced, then proceeded to drain the glass of lemonade Peggy handed him in one long gulp. "Everybody's calm."

"Hooray!" declared Taylor. "Can I go in?"

Vicky suspected the answer, but let Nick deliver the news. He squatted down next to Taylor, not quite hiding a wince when he did so. Every time he aggravated his knee by getting down to Taylor's height warmed her heart. "I know you want to," he said softly. "But they aren't ready for you just yet. Tomorrow, I promise. But they went through a lot today. I need to borrow your mom, though. Dunk has a scratch from all the commotion and I know you'd want us to be sure he's okay."

Taylor's lower lip started to quiver. He'd been waiting a long time to make sure his barn friends were okay. This was just going to be a tough outcome for Taylor.

Nick caught the level of Taylor's disappointment. "Tell you what. Your mom and I will take you up to the barn door to look, but you can't go inside. You'll have to come back here while your mom and I go inside. Can you do that for me? For Buddy and Dunk?"

Taylor's okay was tiny and near tears, but he agreed. Nick put his hand out for a shake, but Taylor simply grabbed it, then grabbed Vicky's hand and started walking as if the trio of them was the most natural thing in the world.

Leap of faith indeed.

Nick hurt just about everywhere. Still, the extraordinary wonder of walking toward the barn with Taylor holding his hand brought back all the power of the earlier truck ride. His affection for Taylor officially slipped beyond his control, helpless as he was to resist how easily the boy accepted him. How much he needed that acceptance.

Buddy and Dunk were in the far corner of the pen, close together. The continual movement had stopped. He suspected the animals were as spent as he was.

"See 'em?" he asked Taylor. "They're quiet now."

"So they're not scared anymore?" Taylor asked.

"Well, I expect we'll need to keep the dogs away from them for a while and be careful about how they get together when they do. After a while, they'll be good friends, though. Buddy and Dunk know they're safe here, and that's what matters."

"I can't pet them like I used to?" Disappointment filled the little guy's blue eyes.

"Just not yet," Vicky answered for him.

"But they're okay?" Taylor persisted.

"That's why I have to go look at Dunk's scratch. To be sure."

"Does he need a Donkey Band-Aid?"

Nick had to laugh. He felt like he needed a dozen Band-

Aids himself. "If he does, we've got your mom to make it happen."

"Go on back under the tree now and finish those cookies," Vicky told her son. "I'll just be a minute. You've done a great job today."

With one reluctant last look toward his friends, Taylor darted back across the field to where Cay and Peggy were waiting.

"He's got a great big heart for such a little guy," Nick said.

"He's the best thing about my life," Vicky replied with a sigh.

Taylor had become one of the best things about Nick's life. How had that happened so quickly?

"Let's check Dunk out," Vicky said. "It's that right front leg, isn't it?"

Nick nodded toward the red streak marring the gray coat on Dunk's leg. "Buddy came down on him by accident. He's not favoring it, but I don't know how deep the cut is." He caught a bit of fear in Vicky's eyes. "They're calm enough to get close to now." And then, before he could stop himself, he added, "I'll make sure you're safe."

The urge to make sure Vicky and Taylor were safe, to do the thing his darker thoughts hounded him that he hadn't done with Roger, pounded in his chest like a constant drum. Almost since the first day. It had become something beyond the need to redeem himself. It had become genuine care.

"Hi there, Buddy," Nick said as they walked closer. "Mind if we take a look at Dunk here?" Buddy paced a bit as they walked close, but nothing that served as a warning sign. Still, Nick kept talking in a low and soothing voice, coming at the animal from the side by his shoulder so Buddy could see them clearly as they approached. "You remember Vicky, right?"

"I've got a treat for you and Dunk," Vicky offered, remembering the apples Cay had handed her before starting toward the barn. "I know you both like those."

She kept her palm out and flat as Buddy's big lips gingerly scooped up the first two slices.

Dunk, never one to lose out on the opportunity for treats, came right up to her looking for his own snack.

"You, too, fella. But you have to let me look at that leg if you want these." After offering an apple slice, Vicky gently touched Dunk's leg. Then she slowly lifted it as she hunched down over the wound. Buddy moved a bit closer, ready to stand guard over his smaller companion.

"Nothing to worry about," Nick said to Buddy. "We like her, remember?" It struck him how true the statement was.

With a practiced set of motions, Vicky opened her bag and removed things to treat the wound. "It's not deep," she remarked with relief. "Just some antibiotic gel and a bandage for a day or two and you'll be as good as new."

With Dunk on one side and Buddy on the other, Nick kept a hand on Buddy's halter and alternated patting each animal's neck. "See," he assured them, "just like I said. Nothing to worry about. All that funny business earlier is over and done with. Nothing but good days ahead of us now."

He was grateful Vicky was following his cue of a steady stream of calm words. Being a vet, she was a natural at this, but there was something about her voice that called to him. He wanted to hear her talk to him in those tones. If there was a more dangerous thought than that, he didn't know what it was.

"Everybody's in good shape," she pronounced as she secured Dunk's bandage and put things back in her bag.

As she came around in front of Dunk, the donkey pushed off to one side, sending Vicky falling toward Nick, where he stood between the two animals. Nick's reaction was instant. Wary of Buddy's reaction to the sudden movement, he grabbed her and pulled her to his chest, angling himself against Buddy to keep Vicky safe.

Remarkably, Buddy didn't react. A bit of surprise, but not of threat. In fact, Dunk moved closer as if the pair had conspired to get him and Vicky into the tight spot.

Having her within the protection of his arms startled him, but it was a good startle. As if something he'd been trying to ignore just demanded his attention.

He tried to tell himself it was just frayed nerves, just a reaction to the stress and challenge of the past few hours. But it wasn't. And the urge to keep Vicky safe went beyond a successful animal rescue. In fact, Nick was pretty sure it wasn't about the animals anymore. Perhaps it never was.

Buddy and Dunk, stubborn conspirators that they were, didn't move. Dunk made a noise that sounded way too much like a low laugh while Nick could have sworn Buddy offered a "What? Who, me?" look.

It had to have only been a few seconds, but the contact seemed to halt time. Nick noticed everything all at once. The way the streaks of sunshine coming in through the slats in the barn wall hit her hair. The quick cadence of her breath. How she felt delicate and strong at the same time. The unbelievable, irrational sense of grounding he felt holding her. As if the world had been spiraling around him for the past years, and he suddenly found something solid to grab onto.

Did she feel it? It seemed absurd to think so, and yet he

sensed something more than sheer startle in her. Did she hesitate to pull away, or was that his imagination?

It seemed like an hour before Nick managed to find his voice and say—with nowhere near the calm he was hoping—"Hey boys, you wanna let up on the vise grip here?"

Rather an odd comment, since the last thing Nick wanted to do was let up on the grasp he had on Vicky. The way she'd fallen, Vicky was toward the rear of the animals, so she couldn't move, given how walking behind a startled horse was never smart. So it was up to Nick, Buddy, or Dunk to provide an escape from their current predicament.

"Dunk," Vicky said, "Could you move, please?"

Nick thought he heard the same failing attempt to be casual that had marked his own words. "Big pen," he said, just to fill in the awkward silence. "Lotsa room here. Be nice to the doc." He thought if he used her name, the word *Vicky* would come out sounding like the tangle of feelings knotting in his chest at the moment.

Finally, after what felt like an unbearably long time, Dunk gave his characteristic bray and walked away as if nothing had happened at all.

Something definitely had happened.

Nick just couldn't say what exactly.

Chapter Thirteen

Vicky and Meg sat on a pair of porch chairs in front of Vicky's house on Sunday afternoon after church services were done. Grant had some business to attend to, so Vicky took advantage of the chance to spend some time with her friend while their children played. Watching Taylor play with Tabitha and Sadie always soothed Vicky. So few places felt spacious in her life, open and honest and kind. Her time with Meg was one of those precious places.

Today, as the trio of children played some made-up circle game, giggling in the sun, Vicky felt safe enough to ask the question that had pressed on her since the time in the barn yesterday.

"When did you know it was time?" Vicky put a hand to her heart, hoping to convey the thought she couldn't quite put words to yet.

Meg lowered one eyebrow. "Time to what?" And then as her gaze strayed to Vicky's hand—the one no longer wearing a wedding band now resting over her heart—understanding warmed the woman's eyes. "Oh, *that* when."

It felt so vulnerable to even voice the question. All night Vicky seemed to bounce back and forth between too soon, and it's been so long. Where was the turning point between grieving and lonely?

Vicky was grateful Meg didn't answer quickly, but gave the idea some thought. "I suppose if you ask every widow in High Mountain, you'd get a different answer."

"But it's different with us," Vicky insisted. "We're younger, with children. It's not the same as Aunt Cay or any of them." She suddenly found that a judgmental thing to say. "It's not that their loss is bigger or smaller, it's just… different." She winced at her own inability to put this into the right words.

"You're right," Meg replied. "It is different with us. Even Cay or any of them would agree with that. Every family seems incomplete with someone gone, but we feel the hole far bigger, I think. And then there's the whole 'keep it together on account of the kids' thing. Crying in the shower, am I right?"

Vicky felt her eyes pop. "I thought I was the only one who did that."

Meg's smile was as warm as the summer sunshine. "Oh, no, ma'am. You are far from the only one."

Of course Meg understood. "So how do you know?"

Meg sighed. "Well, all I can tell you is that I didn't know. I didn't even know *how* I'd know, actually. For the longest time, all I could see was the struggle. There didn't seem to be room for anything else."

That sounded so familiar it made Vicky's chest ache. "And then?"

"Then a litter of puppies appeared out my back door and a giant, grumpy man came through my front door."

Practically the whole town knew the story of the abandoned puppies that launched Three Sisters Rescue Farm and Grant's initial opposition to the whole idea. It was almost amusing how Vicky had seen her cousin slowly fall for Meg, fighting it the whole way. She felt safe to ask, "Did it feel wrong? At first?"

It struck her that she'd not even named what—or who—she was talking about. It made her pulse hitch to realize she didn't need to. Could Meg see it? Whatever it was growing between her and Nick? The very idea made her want to hide.

"It didn't feel safe, that's for sure." Meg shifted in her chair. "*Wrong*'s not the word I'd use. But there wasn't the thread connecting Grant and Andy the way things connect Nick and Roger. That's a pretty big complication."

Relief at being able to talk about this with someone warred with the exposed feeling pulling Vicky's chest tight. "It should be wrong, shouldn't it?" Vicky asked.

"It is, and it isn't. What feels wrong?" Meg questioned, more curiosity than judgment in her tone.

"I've spent all this time with my version of what I think happened the day Roger was shot. Boxed in by my grief and anger. Determined not to accept the official reports because there could be nothing right or just in how Roger died."

Meg turned to look out across the lawn to where the three children were playing. "There isn't anything right or just in a father dying while his children are so small. You know it. I know it. It's wrong on every kind of level."

Vicky pulled her knees up onto the chair and hugged them. "You ever heard the saying two things can be true at the same time?"

"Sure."

"My resentment and Nick's story are both true. He sees himself as guilty for not overriding the procedures. I mean, he did what he should have done, but Roger died like he shouldn't have." Those last words still cut edges into her heart. "I was so sure I knew the whole story, so set in my anger against Nick, that I wouldn't see it from his point of view."

"And now?" Meg had sensed a change in her. She'd said so. That was Meg—there was little hope of hiding much from the woman's keen observational gifts.

"Now that I do, it's like those two true things cancel each other out. I can't hate him anymore. That feels strange and… I don't know…off-balance. Like there's a hole in me where all that resentment used to be." She looked at Meg. "Does that make any sense?"

Meg shook her head. "I don't think these things ever make much sense. Not in the logical way." She gave Vicky a direct look. "But they make sense in other illogical ways." She touched her heart.

Vicky felt like she was falling off-balance. "I don't know if what's going on inside me is real or just the fallout from all that anger going away."

Meg pulled an animal cracker from the box they'd set out for the kids to snack on. "Didn't you just tell me about two things being true at the same time?"

"So it could be real even if it is partly from the anger going away? I can't just flip a switch from hating him to… to…" She couldn't even bring herself to name the warm glow that had followed her around since that moment in the barn. The echo of Nick's off-pitch voice and the sight of his hand wrapped around Taylor's stayed with her constantly. The overwhelming sense of protection she'd felt when he pressed against her. If she didn't know any better, she'd have sworn Buddy and Dunk conspired to push them together like that. Which was absurd. Wasn't it?

Meg did what Meg often did—got straight to the point. "Are you asking me if it's okay to feel something for Nick?"

It was more than a little unsettling to have it put so

bluntly. "I suppose I am." There. She'd said it out loud. Admitted to someone—the only person in High Mountain who might truly understand—what was going on in her heart.

Meg finished the cookie as she touched the ring on her left hand. "The fact that I'm married to Grant Emerson should tell you all you need to know about that. I didn't see it coming. Not in a million years. And it scared me to death at first." She caught Vicky's gaze. "But it's been blessing upon blessing. I never thought I'd be this happy again. And the girls? Grant is God's gift to their little lives. Every day. And God's gift to me." Meg waved her hand in a dismissive gesture. "Look at me, gushing like a greeting card."

"It's nice," Vicky said, truly meaning it. "I want to be that happy again."

Meg reached in for another cracker. "What is it about him? Aside from all the history you have, I mean. As a person, as a man, what do you see?"

"That's just it—I can't set aside the history. It's like we have two versions of the same wound. We both lost Roger. In very different ways—I get that—but we still share it."

"He's great with Taylor," Meg offered. "Even I can see that. And Taylor adores him."

Vicky thought again of the time in the truck. How could such a crisis situation turn itself into a precious memory? "Despite how I balked at him, those two connected almost instantly. I didn't trust that at first. I thought Nick might be using him to get to me."

"I was worried about that, too. But Nick is genuine about wanting to set things right with you. Sounds like he has." Meg leaned closer. "But it sounds as if it might go farther than that." She paused before adding, "Vicky, it wouldn't be a terrible thing if you found yourself feeling things—true, new things—about Nick. In fact, it might be an amazing thing. A whopping, God-sized wonder."

Vicky stared straight at her wise friend. "That's exactly what I'm afraid of."

Thursday had been set as the big day. Vicky and Taylor traveled to Three Sisters Farm for Taylor's first attempt to ride Dunk.

"Okay," Nick said with all the authority he could muster and still be kind, "We're going to try this today. You have to listen very carefully and do everything just like I say. Deal?"

"That's extra important today," Vicky added. "You do like Mr. Nick says."

Taylor nodded with such solemnity that it sank straight into Nick's heart. He'd been working with Dunk all week, brushing him, slipping blankets, packs, and saddles on for short stretches, making extraordinary progress. So much progress that he was daring to believe Wally's insistence that God really was working a wonder here. It defied belief that Nick could create this much trust and acceptance in an animal with Dunk's and Buddy's history in the short span of a month. And yet it had happened,

And it also just so happened that Dunk was too small to carry an adult rider just yet. That made Taylor just the right size. And Taylor wanted it more than anything. Funny enough, Dunk seemed to want it, too.

That was both good and bad. Nick had to take extra care and every precaution for the good of both Dunk and Taylor. But if there was ever a perfect match for a donkey and a boy, this was it. Dunk was eager to please and had taken walks around the farm with some light loads to test his growing strength.

Taylor pointed to Dunk's nose where a leather strap sat. "*D-U-N-K*. That's Dunk. That's his name."

"It is," Vicky replied.

One of the farm supporters—the same one who had made leather collars for all the first litter of dogs—had made halters for both Buddy and Dunk. Somehow, it felt like their official citizenship card at Three Sisters Rescue Farm.

Nick held up the pad he'd been easing onto Dunk's back for the past few days. "He's had this pad and the saddle on him a couple of times now. But you gotta go careful. Donkeys and horses are persnickety about their backs." He'd chosen the word *persnickety* half because he knew Taylor would find it funny, and half because it was a better way to talk about how horses instinctually knew predators often attacked their backs and necks. It's what made saddle training such a tricky business.

True to prediction, Taylor laughed at the silly-sounding word. "What's periskidy mean?" His mispronunciation charmed Nick.

"Same as how you don't like me washing the back of your knees," Vicky offered with a soft smile. She smiled more often each time they were together. He liked that. Perhaps it was part of God's extraordinary progress, too.

Nick eased the saddle onto Dunk, pleased at how the donkey accepted the tack with calm ease. Taylor was trying hard to keep a lid on his impatience to ride Dunk. The barely hidden eagerness was just about the cutest thing Nick had ever seen. He could tell the stretch of time it took to cinch all the straps and buckles felt like forever to the little guy. Still, Nick took the time to double-check everything. This had to be perfect.

When he was satisfied Dunk was ready and the tack

was secure, Nick turned to Vicky and nodded. This felt like a big moment. Sure, it was just a matter of Nick leading Dunk around the small pen with both adults close by, but it was coming to mean so much more. He chose this moment to try out a new nickname for Taylor. "You ready, Horsey Boy?"

Nick first watched Vicky's reaction. After a moment of surprise, she grinned. After all, Taylor had persisted in calling Nick the Horsey Man. This gave them something to share, hopefully.

Taylor's reaction was instantaneous. Nick felt he could live to be a hundred and never forget the brilliance of that grin. "Yep!" he nearly shouted.

Vicky buckled the chin strap on Taylor's pint-sized riding helmet, then gestured a "go ahead" to Nick. The sense of validation and victory Nick felt as he hoisted Taylor onto Dunk's back defied description. It felt silly to feel as if everything in the past few years had been leading up to this moment, but that's how he truly felt. As if he lifted far more than one small boy. He lifted his life. Raised his hope for what might lie ahead.

Dunk, thankfully, was a perfect gentleman. He'd planned for this to be a short experiment of a ride. Nick wanted no chance for anything to go wrong or to frighten boy or beast. Everyone needed this to be a victory.

Catching Vicky's expression out of the corner of his eye as they made a slow loop of the pen, Nick knew she needed the victory, too. They'd never talked about it, but she needed to be able to put her faith in something and not have it pulled out from beneath her.

Walking Dunk and Taylor across the pen, seeing the sheer glee in Taylor's eyes, Nick knew he wanted Vicky to be able to put her faith in him.

He'd never be able to explain how, but the way Dunk's big brown eyes caught his gaze, Nick was certain Dunk put his faith in him as well. After shouldering so much blame for so long, it felt as if the world settled into the right place with the loops they made around the pen.

"Look at me, Mommy!"

Was there a more heartwarming thing in the world?

"Look at you, Taylor," Vicky called back. Nick could hear the catch of tears in her voice. His own throat felt tight with the sense of redemption that practically filled the room.

"You're doing great, pal," Nick encouraged. "Keep your hands on the pommel," he said, pointing to the knob at the front of the saddle. "And your eyes looking ahead."

"Good job, Dunk," Taylor cheered. "We walk good together."

Nick could easily imagine leading Taylor and Dunk down the street at the pet parade. In fact, his eagerness to do so stunned him. If anything happened to make that too much of a risk, he'd be as disappointed as Taylor. Maybe more. But he also knew he would do anything—even disappoint Taylor, himself, the whole town—to keep that little boy safe. He cared so much for Taylor that it scared him.

He was coming to care a great deal for Vicky, too, and that scared him even more. Even if he did manage to set things right with Vicky and Taylor, walking out of High Mountain was going to be the hardest thing he'd ever do. If his knee injury didn't confine him to a desk job, even going back to the lonely ranger existence in the U.S. Field and Wildlife Service would feel like a punishment.

"One more lap, okay?" he said, even though his heart wanted more time in the wonder of this moment.

"Just one?" Taylor whined. "Can't I have more?"

He knew exactly how Taylor felt. "We gotta take it slow. For Dunk. He hasn't had many little boys sit on his back before."

In fact, Nick was pretty sure Dunk had never been ridden ever. Still, the donkey seemed to sense the importance of his role here. He'd adapted far beyond Nick's expectations, and far faster. He knew what Pastor Jim and Wally and even Cay might have to say about that.

The thing was, he was starting to believe it, too.

As they finished the last loop, Nick saw Vicky standing next to Buddy. They were watching Dunk and Taylor together. And when Vicky put her hand gently on Buddy's neck, the horse turned toward her as if to say, *I know. I see it, too.*

Nick brought Dunk and Taylor to the side of the pen. "All done for today. Get ready to swing the leg farthest from me up and over when I lift you up, okay?"

Taylor's nod wobbled the helmet on his head in the most adorable way. "Got it."

It was as if the boy weighed nothing at all. There was no effort in raising him off the saddle. But when Taylor reached up and clung to Nick's neck, giggling with happiness, Horsey Man to Horsey Boy, this hug felt like it changed the world. Mostly because, to him, it did.

"I like riding Dunk," Taylor said into Nick's neck, not loosening up on the grip he had.

Nick found it hard to speak. "I think Dunk likes you riding him. You guys make a great team."

Taylor pulled back to look into Nick's face, and Nick felt his heart break wide open. "Do you get to ride him next?"

Technically, Dunk might be able to support a man of Nick's size. But it wasn't necessary, plus it was far beyond what Dunk could manage at the moment. Besides,

Nick felt the crazy urge to keep Dunk just for Taylor. At least for now. "Nah, I think you're just the right size rider for him." Taylor deserved something like this just for him. The chance to be a little hero in front of the whole town.

"You're sure?" Taylor asked as Nick finally managed to set him down. "It's fun. He's bumpy."

It was an unusual way to describe a donkey's walk, but it worked. "He is, isn't he?" Nick allowed himself to touch Taylor's chin, tipping it up toward him. Vicky noticed. And she didn't seem to mind. After all, Taylor had started it with that tiny-whopper of a hug. "I think he deserves a treat for all that hard work, don't you?"

"We both do," Taylor replied with a hopeful expression. After all, what was a visit to Three Sisters Farm without a visit to Aunt Cay's kitchen for something yummy? Besides, Nick wanted a moment alone with Vicky to process what had just happened. He wanted a moment alone with Vicky, period. He wanted a long dinner watching the sun go down, or an hour looking up at the stars. Or even ten minutes getting lost in her eyes.

Getting lost? He was lost already. He knew that. He just had no idea what to do about it. Or how to recover if the answer—which he suspected it was—was do nothing about it.

He looked to Vicky over Taylor's head, seeking a clue as to whether she'd agree to sending her son into the big house in search of treats. He told himself what she did next would tell him how to go from here.

To Nick's surprise, she held his gaze while she replied, "I'm pretty sure Auntie Cay has an apple in the kitchen she'll cut in half for Dunk. And maybe a cookie for you."

"You guys want a cookie, too?" Taylor asked. The boy's

natural generosity was such an amazing thing. Nick left it to Vicky to answer.

"I think we're good," Vicky said, still holding Nick's gaze. He wondered if her eyes really said everything he thought they did. He didn't trust his judgment right now. He was entirely too hopeful for his own good.

Chapter Fourteen

How had they gotten to this place?

Vicky felt so many different emotions as she heard Taylor's boots dash out of the barn toward the big house and his Auntie Cay.

They shouldn't be here, looking at each other the way they were. Trying not to feel what she knew—deep down knew—Nick was feeling as strongly as she.

He cared.

It was in every word he spoke to Taylor, every way he acted with him, everything he did with Buddy and Dunk.

What was she supposed to do with that? With the way it shifted her world? With the hum under her skin that defied logic?

Vicki started with the one thing she knew for sure. "Taylor's over the moon to ride Dunk. This might be the happiest I've been since..." Suddenly that felt like the worst possible thing to say. "...in a long while," she finished. They both knew what she'd avoided saying.

"You can say it," Nick said. "It's the happiest I've been since Roger died, too." He looked both ashamed and relieved at the admission.

And there was the astounding truth of it all: they were climbing out of this valley together.

Nick scratched his chin. "He's so amazing, Taylor. I forgot there was that much joy in the world, you know?"

"Some days he's the only thing that keeps me going." She sat on one of the hay bales, the wonder of the past half hour making her almost dizzy. "Oh, everybody tells me how great I'm doing, how strong I am, all that stuff."

Nick took a few steps toward her, and the dizzy feeling returned. "It's true. I think you're the strongest person I know. Taylor's so lucky to have you. Even when you feel like a mess, remember that." He took another few steps and sat down on the hay bale next to hers. It felt too close and not close enough at the same time. "Look at me, talking like that. I feel like a mess most days." He gazed down at her, his brown eyes looking warm and dark. Deep, like something that went on forever. And clear. The way pain makes everything clear, everything sharp.

"You weren't a mess the day you handled Buddy and Dunk with the dogs," she offered. "Did you know Taylor called you the Hero Horsey Man that night?"

Nick laughed at that. "I'm the farthest thing from a hero."

A notion rose up from deep inside Vicky. One so unexpected, so powerful, it hit her like a gust of wind. She could be part of Nick's healing. His presence here had been all about what he'd done to her, what he wanted from her. Never had she thought about what *she* could give *him*. The forgiveness was obvious—and she was working hard on that—but it could go farther.

Redemption. Perhaps the most amazing outcome of this whole unlikely situation was redemption. For Nick, yes, but it would overflow to her and Taylor, too. Suddenly it wasn't about forcing herself to do the hard spiritual work of forgiving Nick. It was about stepping into the astounding emotional gift of redeeming him.

She could do that. She wanted to do that.

"Nick," she began, unsure how to move forward but knowing she would find a way.

His eyes fell closed at his name. If it wasn't the first time she'd said his name, it was the first time she'd said it with tenderness.

"I'm glad you're here." A simple sentence, but it seemed to encompass all of what was going on between them.

He looked up at the barn ceiling, and Vicky saw the emotions play across his face in huge waves. "You don't know what it does to me to hear you say that," he choked out.

Only she did know. It was in his face, in the thick emotion around his words, in the way his hands fisted and his breath hitched.

"I think maybe I do," she managed. Some hard shell, one that had been around her heart for so long she'd hardly remembered it was there, broke open and started to fall away.

He looked at her again, and a long-forgotten sense of falling swept over her. *Him. The last person I'd ever imagine.* She wanted to stay very quiet and laugh out loud at the same time. Vicky thought about taking his hand, but that felt like too much. Instead, she laid her hand on the hay bale an inch or so from his. They were going to have to take this in such tiny steps. There was so much to work through, so many deep valleys to traverse.

"I can't bring him back," Nick said softly, his voice almost cracking.

It was so true. Part of her wanted someone to blame for what had happened to Roger. But Nick was right. No one could bring Roger back. And she knew now, in a way she hadn't before, that Nick had not taken Roger away from them.

"No one can bring him back," she said. Vicky found herself able to take the huge step that was needed here. "And I don't blame you. Anymore. Oh, I did, for a long time, but I was wrong. I forgive you, but I know now there was nothing to forgive."

"There was," he cut in. "I could have..."

Vicky chose that moment to put her hand on his, silencing his protest. "No, you couldn't have," she refuted, surprised at how much she truly meant it. "Roger made choices. Things no one could have predicted happened. We both live with what happened. I think if you forgive me, and I forgive you, then maybe we have someplace to start. Start over. Start new." She offered him a smile and gave his hand the slightest squeeze. His hand was toughened by work, strong, but warm. "This is *our* last twenty feet. Now we go on from here."

It was a bit of a speech, but all of it needed to be said.

Nick looked at her hand on his as if he couldn't quite believe she'd touched him. He turned his palm over so that her hand rested inside his instead of on top of it. Vicky marveled at the image—his tanned hand beneath her pale one. They fit. It was an odd thing to think, but then again maybe not. It struck as deep a chord in her as the sight of Taylor's hand in Nick's, back when the pickup truck raced toward the barn. Somehow that felt so long ago.

Slowly, carefully, Nick raised his hand as it held hers. He folded his other hand on top of hers, enveloping it. He touched it as if it were the most precious thing in all the world. How long had it been since someone had held her hand? Taylor had, of course, but this was different in a thousand ways. The rightness of it shook every part of her. And yet it also settled a million things into place.

"Where do we go from here?" he asked, referring to her

earlier words. "I don't know how to do this." After a pause, he added, "I don't know if we should."

Vicky's answer came lightly, easily, and honestly. "Me, neither."

"But you want to try." The disbelief in Nick's voice sent a pang through her.

"Yes." One word that broke open a host of possibilities. Scary ones, big ones, but important ones. Ones she'd denied herself for a long time.

"You're sure?" He was giving her every opportunity to back away. There was something so honorable in that. A humility and care that called to her and made her feel safe. When was the last time she felt safe?

"Of course I'm not sure," she replied with a laugh that bubbled up from some newly lightened place deep inside.

He kept the tender grip on her hand. It gave her an anchor in the spinning, shifting world of what they were considering. "Well, that makes two of us. I don't think I've ever been less sure of anything." Still, his touch spoke of surety even if his words held all the uncertainty she felt.

"Maybe that's how this goes."

They were talking in circles, babbling like dumbstruck teenagers instead of the life-weary adults they were. And still the lightness of it, the giddy possibility, hung in the air.

Vicky reached out with her other hand, so that her hand now rested atop his. They were both staring at their joined hands, both reaching for the right thing to say and coming up woefully short.

"I got treats!" Taylor's announcement came from the open barn door, breaking the hush of the moment. Nick and Vicky yanked their hands apart, each of them jumping up off the hay bales. She prayed Taylor wouldn't catch on to everything that had happened in his absence. Of course, he likely had no idea, but the vulnerability of the moment felt as if it were flashing like a neon sign. Vicky had an absurd moment of gratitude that Buddy and Dunk couldn't talk. What would those two say about what had just happened?

"I got apples for Dunk and Buddy. And cookies for us."

When Vicky raised an eyebrow at Taylor's chocolate-smeared cheeks, Taylor added, "I ate mine already, but here's yours." Taylor deposited an enormous chocolate chip cookie in Vicky's hand, then Nick's.

"You're sure I don't get the apples and they get the cookie?" Nick asked with a hint of playfulness Vicky couldn't ever remember hearing in his voice.

"No, silly." Taylor giggled as he walked off toward the pen fence where Dunk and Buddy stood ready to snack.

Nick shrugged, grinned, and took a bite of cookie as he followed Taylor toward the animals.

Something important had shifted. For everyone in the barn.

Chapter Fifteen

The next morning, Vicky finished up an exam for a family's new puppy and walked out into the veterinary office lobby to find her mom and two aunts waiting. Aunt Peggy was holding a stack of posters for the pet parade. All three of the sisters, however, were wearing the sort of conspiratorial grin Vicky had come to recognize.

Something was up.

Perhaps it wasn't the best idea to tell Mom about what had happened in the barn yesterday. Still, she'd wanted her mother's reaction to the still-surprising idea that there could be something between her and Nick. Gather a few gentle encouragers, as it were, before things went any further.

Mom had been remarkably supportive. She easily accepted that Vicky had rushed to blame Nick, that their hard conversation about what had really happened that day was long overdue and necessary.

Much to Vicky's surprise, Mom had already picked up on the growing connection she had with Nick. Taylor's instant bond was so obvious that everyone saw it. And while Vicky had hoped to hide the inexplicable pull she felt toward Nick for a bit longer, it helped to hear her mother's view.

Still, Vicky had neglected one vital fact: Mom wouldn't

keep this to herself. Her aunts would know instantly. And it was sheer foolishness to expect the three McNally sisters not to meddle the minute they knew.

Poor Nick. He had no idea what might be about to hit him.

"We're putting up parade posters," Aunt Cay announced. "How many do you want?"

"Five," Vicky replied as she handed the puppy's file back to her receptionist. "Two for up front and one for each of the exam rooms." That might be a bit overboard, but she truly wanted the parade to be a huge success. For Taylor, Dunk, Nick, the farm, and the whole town. Taylor talked of nothing else, and was fixated on riding Dunk through town as the Horsey Boy. In truth, after yesterday Vicky cherished the image of walking down High Mountain's main street on one side of Dunk with Taylor in the saddle and Nick on the other side.

"That's even more than Meg took at the diner." Mom beamed. "Good for you."

"Have you got any pets registered already?" While walk-up entries would definitely be welcomed, Mom had agreed to Vicky's suggestion that someone gather a list of expected pets and their owners. After all, it might help to know if there were dogs that needed to be kept far from cats, cats that needed to be well away from birds, and any other interspecies conflicts that could occur. Anything that could ensure this would be a fun celebration for everyone was a good idea.

"Sixteen," Mom replied. Her eyes squinted as she attempted to pull up the collection in her memory, ticking the count off on her fingers. "Four dogs, three cats, a bird, a pair of chickens, a turtle, two rabbits, and a goldfish."

"A regular Noah's ark," Peggy joked. "Minus the flood, of course."

"Do we have a rain plan?" Vicky asked. No rain was forecast for the day so far, but mountain weather could change on a dime.

"Our rain plan is everyone gets wet," said Cay with a smirk. "Except the fish. He's already wet."

"Our fish is a lady," Mom corrected. "Gladys the Goldfish. But I expect the cats won't take to rain one bit."

Vicky could just imagine half a dozen wet cats yowling their way down the street. "What if we got permission to use the high school gymnasium?" she suggested. "We'd be looping around like a racetrack, sure, but I think it would still be fun." It lit a small glow under her ribs to be talking about something so happy and community-filled as this parade. She had put herself on the sidelines for too long. Mom had said as much last night. It was scary to step back into the world like this, but also exhilarating.

Cay elbowed her sister. "You raised such a smart woman, Barb."

Mom's smile warmed with a mother's pride.

"Oh, and don't forget the donkey," Barb added. "We can't not count Dunk. After all, he's the star of the show." She beamed. "And my grandson is riding him." There was something to be said for a grandmother's pride, too.

"I saw Taylor riding Dunk yesterday at the farm," Cay said. "Sweetest thing ever." She caught Vicky's eye. "That Nick has worked wonders, hasn't he?"

Vicky tried to answer without giving away any of the emotion attached to her answer.

When the aunts exchanged knowing looks with each other, Vicky knew she hadn't quite succeeded. There was no hiding things from the McNally sisters.

But in truth, Nick *had* worked wonders. In the one session Nick had done with Taylor riding Dunk, the two had become a clever little team. She had no doubt that Taylor's confidence as a rider would grow along with Dunk's readiness to be ridden. It was as if they gave the gift of partnership to each other.

The poignancy of that—and how it mirrored her own growing closeness to Nick—wasn't lost on her. Never in a million years did Vicky imagine this was how the healing of her heart would happen. It was as perfect as it was surprising. What was it Pastor Jim said about God being in the surprise business?

"By the way, we were wondering…" Peggy started.

Here it comes, Vicky mused. It was obvious the trio was here for more than poster placement.

"Are you free for dinner tomorrow night?" Peggy continued. "At the farm? It looks like it's going to be such a lovely evening."

Having a Saturday night out sounded rather inviting. Even if it did come with a side dish of McNally sister meddling. Vicky chose to play along. "Just me?"

"Oh, Taylor of course." Peggy made a poor attempt of just getting an idea. "But I think Nick said he'd be finishing up the fence tomorrow. If we have any extra, I'm sure every bachelor appreciates a good home-cooked meal."

Ah, there it is.

For all the blatant meddling, Vicky found she couldn't bring herself to be annoyed. It felt like a new step, being around Nick in the evening, sharing a meal. But it felt like a welcome one. And with the aunts and Taylor around, it certainly wouldn't be anything close to a date. She wasn't ready for that, not yet.

"That'd be lovely, thank you."

Mission accomplished, the aunts deposited the posters on the counter and waved a cheerful goodbye on their way out the door. Whether or not they were truly going around town hanging posters, or had just used that as an excuse to come into the office, Vicky didn't know.

To her surprise, she didn't care. She'd said a cautious prayer this morning that God would show her what the next step with Nick ought to be.

Here was her answer.

She shook her head and gave a small laugh as she peered through the office's front windows to watch the aunts bustle down the street. No doubt about it, the McNally sisters were a force to be reckoned with. Some days her mother and her sisters irritated Vicky to no end. Other days, they came equipped with solutions no one saw coming.

She turned back toward the reception counter to find her receptionist, Gloria, staring at her with a dubious expression. "Did I just witness a setup?"

Vicky had been careful not to mention any of this in the veterinary office. "I think so," she admitted.

"He is awfully handsome," Gloria offered. "And Taylor adores him." She knew enough of the history to ask, "Can you work through all the stuff between you?"

"So far, yes." Vicky hugged her chest. "But there's a lot of stuff. I still don't know where this is going."

"Maybe you don't have to just yet. Don't you always tell owners not to borrow tomorrow's problems today?"

It always stung a little bit to have your own advice used against you. "I do say that, don't I?"

Every movement forward—for her, for Nick, for Buddy, for Dunk, and for Taylor—had happened in small steps.

Maybe it was the right time to take a bigger one.

Her next appointment, a cranky cat with a tooth infection, came through the door in the arms of his worried owner. Her next step with Nick would, as she'd so often counseled, have to be tomorrow's problem.

Nick nailed the last bit of fencing to the final post just as the sun started to set in the sky on Saturday. He'd kept his promise. The fence was finished and ready for whenever Buddy and Dunk were settled enough to roam the full farm freely.

It hadn't come cheap, but it was more than worth it. Peggy, Cay, and Barb would be able to take in "whatever critters God sends next," as they liked to say. It'd probably be good if God didn't send anything larger than Buddy, he mused. No bulls, cows, that sort of thing.

His conversations with God came surprisingly easy out here in the fields. His faith grew with the length of the fence, it seemed. Nick confessed all his grief and regret, finding that the darkness slowly gave way to hope. *I came here to set things right. And You knew the thing I most needed to set right was myself, Lord. I'm grateful.*

When he walked away from High Mountain—and Nick was trying hard not to think about that—he would now have healing no one could take away from him. Healing that had nothing to do with his knee.

He'd told the three sisters that the final stretch of fence would be done today, and they'd invited him to supper to celebrate. As he put away his tools, Nick reached for the clean shirt and the extra water and washcloth he'd stashed in the truck cab. It wouldn't do to appear for dinner as the sweaty mess he currently was.

Nick had just dried off and buttoned his shirt when he saw Vicky's vehicle come over the ridge. His heart did that flip it had begun to do whenever she was near. His hand could remember the softness of her fingers against his palm. He seemed to carry the surprised warmth in her eyes all the time, mirroring what he felt inside. He'd not asked, but secretly hoped Vicky might be invited to tonight's dinner as well.

She wore a bright green dress he'd once seen her wear to church. Vicky looked more beautiful than ever. Just the right balance of delicate and strong. If he'd had any doubts about how hard he was falling for High Mountain's veterinarian, they were dashed. He was falling. Had already fallen, actually. Hard.

He was surprised to see that Taylor was not with her. And he was downright stunned to see she carried an enormous picnic basket and one of those classic red-and-white-checkered tablecloths. The red of the cloth echoed the slightly bashful pink of her cheeks.

Tonight's dinner would not be what he expected. In a fraction of a second, he connected the dots. This was the work of the legendary McNally sisters meddling. They'd somehow caught on to what was going on between him and Vicky. Since they were obviously endorsing it, Nick found he didn't mind. It was refreshing to have someone in his corner on anything, especially this. A bit more subtlety would have been nice, though.

He tossed everything in the cab and tried to wipe the amused smile off his face. He asked the obvious question. "What's this?"

"Supper," she replied, trying to tamp down her own sheepish amusement.

He reached out and took the basket from her. It was heavy. The sisters had gone all out, it seemed. "I thought supper was at the big house."

"So did I." She tucked a strand of hair behind her ear and

flicked her gaze down for a second. He found the gesture completely endearing. “Seems we’ve been set up.”

Nick was grateful he’d parked his truck near the shade of one of the farm’s enormous spreading oak trees. It was the perfect spot for a sunset picnic. Picturesque. Romantic, even. “I’ve heard that’s a specialty of those three.”

“So is roast chicken,” Vicky said. “And a whole bunch of other stuff, including Aunt Cay’s famous carrot cake.” She nodded toward the basket, which was currently sending up a collection of enticing smells. “There’s a feast in there.”

“Wow.” Not exactly eloquent, but Nick found himself a bit tongue-tied at the prospect of a long stretch of time alone with Vicky.

Vicky spread out the blanket and sat down, motioning to Nick to deposit the basket at one end. Suddenly the space next to Vicky on the blanket pulled him in like gravity. He eased himself down, wildly aware of how little space stretched between them.

He made himself ask, “Where’s Taylor?”

“The sitter Meg and I share has been hired behind my back.”

Nick laughed. “About as subtle as a tornado, those three.” He paused for a moment before adding, “You okay with that?”

“Clearly, I told Mom too much the other night. Usually I have fun watching it done to other people. It’s a bit…much having them set their sights on me.” There was a breathy pause before she added, “Well, us.”

This was different, and they both knew it. Nick chose to lean into it. “Remind me to thank them soon.” He realized his heart was racing and chose the diversion of lifting the basket lid. “Whoa. You weren’t kidding.”

The aunts had gone all out. Fruit, cheese, crackers,

pieces of roasted chicken that set his stomach growling, some sort of salad, bottles of what looked like sparkling lemonade, biscuits, and two gigantic slices of carrot cake. Even paper plates and napkins, as well as plastic glasses and silverware.

He chose to make a joke. "What'd you bring for you to eat?"

She laughed, and the sound of it danced across his skin. He'd only heard her laugh at Taylor. It pleased him that he could make her laugh as well.

Her eyes sparkled as she teased, "Didn't your mother teach you to share?"

She knew so little about him. They were lopsided that way. He knew so much about her and Taylor from Roger's endless conversations, yet she knew next to nothing about his life before the wildlife service. "My mom died when I was slightly older than Taylor. Six. I had a grandma who could put your aunts to shame in the food department, but she passed when I was ten. Most of my life it was just me and Dad."

"I'm sorry. That sounds so hard." He knew the tenderness in her voice was genuine, not the sort of rote reaction his admission often got.

"I got used to my own company. Probably what drew me to working at the wildlife service."

Vicky began pulling out the fruit, cheese, and crackers. "Roger used to say the solitude was the hardest part." She stopped and flushed. "Maybe I shouldn't talk about him."

He put a hand out to touch her wrist. "Don't ever say that. He was part of both our lives. A huge part of yours. And you've tried hard to keep him a part of Taylor's." He took the food from her and clasped her hand in his again, the way he had in the barn. He waited until she looked into his eyes. "We're very different, Roger and I." It had to be said. They had to venture into this with their eyes wide open if they were going to at all.

And he wanted to. Very much. Even if his time here in High Mountain broke his heart for the rest of his days, it felt as if tonight would be worth all of it.

"I know," she replied softly.

The urge to touch her cheek nearly overwhelmed him, but this was a time for caution and patience. It helped that a luxurious dose of time and the sunset spread itself out before them.

He handed her the cheese and took the package of crackers to open them himself. "Do you know how strong you are? Making your way through all this. Making Taylor's way through all of it. He's come through it so well."

Vicky gave a tense laugh. "Looks that good from the outside, does it?"

"I didn't say easy. It isn't. I can see that, if other people can't. But what floors me is the strength. And your compassion. I disappeared and went numb, but you stayed in. Dug your way through it. It's amazing. Astounding even."

She blushed at his flowery words. Usually Vicky was so professional and practical, it delighted him to dole out flowery praise for her. He stopped just sort of saying she was the most amazing woman and mother he'd ever known—mostly because that seemed like too much, even if he felt it.

She took the opened package of crackers from him, and Nick relished how their hands lingered together in the exchange.

"This is all a bit…daunting," she admitted. "I didn't expect…this."

"I'm not even sure I know what this is," he agreed. "But I know I want it. It feels…impossible and right at the same time. Breakable, I suppose. As if one wrong move could shatter a bunch of stuff and hurt people." It was as if all these impassioned words came from some new version of himself he didn't know existed. "But at the same time so much of the hurt is gone. Amazingly gone. Do you feel that?"

He watched her closely. Nick didn't know what he was going to do if she said no.

Chapter Sixteen

"Do you feel that?" he'd asked.

The question pulled at Vicky, as if it reached all the way down inside her. Even if she wanted to deny it, she couldn't. She felt it so strongly she barely knew how to handle it.

The hurt was gone. Almost all of it. There was an echo of pain, like the scent of smoke hanging in the air after a fire, but the flame and the burn were gone. In its place was a glow.

Still, smoldering embers could burn as easily as they glowed. If there was ever a situation where the phrase "playing with fire" applied, it was this. There was no sense in going back, nothing to be gained by refusing to heal. She gave her reply the weight it deserved, holding Nick's gaze as she spoke the words. "Yes, I feel it."

Relief washed over his face. Vicky could almost laugh at how he could have doubted it. It hummed between them. She'd felt it nearly constantly since that first touch in the barn. How could she not?

Nick shook his head, a wonder-filled bafflement in his eyes. His eyes were so dark she would never have said they sparkled, but there was a glint about them now. Something surprisingly close to the joy she loved to see in Taylor's eyes.

"How'd we get here?" he asked.

"We got to the truth." For her, that was the way to explain it. "I needed someone to blame, and I turned you into that person. But you aren't. What happened to Roger happened. And we've both made mistakes in how we dealt with it." She remembered what Meg had asked, about what she saw in Nick as a man aside from their history, and realized there were things he needed to hear. "You're a good man. You are so kind to Taylor. You have a gift with Dunk and Buddy. You know how to pull animals—and people—from dark places."

He shook his head again. "Maybe because I've spent so much time in them myself."

"Maybe. Aunt Cay would tell you that's the whole point of forgiveness and grace. So if you ask me, forgiveness and grace is how we got here."

Nick's eyes grew serious. "I could forgive a dozen people and not feel what I feel about you. And about Taylor. That little boy…he means so much to me." He shifted so that he faced her. "I didn't plan this. You have to know that. I came here to just set things right between us, to make up for how I disappeared. Nothing more than that."

"But it *is* more than that. It's more than just the hurt being gone." She turned his own question back on him. "Do you feel that?"

She could see his helpless-to-deny-it response that had just welled up in her moments ago. "Yeah," he said, the reply more sigh than word. He touched her hand. "I do."

Vicky laced her fingers in his, liking the way her hand felt warm and safe within his. They sat for a moment in silence, too overwhelmed to put the moment into words but too cautious to do anything like move closer to each other.

This was going to take such an enormous, gentle effort. This couldn't be rushed—Nick was right in what he'd said; the wrong move could shatter a bunch of things and hurt people.

And yet, here under the gorgeous open sky, Vicky felt safe and anchored by Nick's hand in hers. What a gift that sense of safety was. She'd felt endangered for so long, teetering on the edge of coping, scrambling to stay functioning and putting on an okay face when she felt anything but.

Not here, and not now. How amazing that Nick, of all people, should make her feel safe. That he, of all people, should be the one to coax her heart back to life.

"Do you remember when I asked you how you know you make progress with a horse?"

Nick's brows furrowed. He didn't yet follow her thinking in asking such a question. "Yeah."

"You said it was when you saw hope in their eyes. When they told you they were ready to trust."

Understanding lit a glow on his features. "I did say that."

Even though her heart pounded, she made herself hold Nick's gaze. She knew she would have to open this door between them. He would wait for however long it took, because that was the kind of man Nick was. He would let the choice be hers.

"What do you see in my eyes?" It felt like the most daring of questions.

"I know what I think I see," he replied. "But, Vicky, I'm gonna need to hear you say it."

"I have hope, Nick. For the first time in such a long time, I have hope. And while it scares me to death, I think I'm ready to trust."

"You're sure?" he asked, a heartwarming disbelief in his tone.

"Of course I'm not sure. Not completely. But sure

enough." The lightness she felt was a nearly giddy sensation. Such an extraordinary change from the weighted, weary version of herself she'd been dragging around inside that shiny shell of coping. "Besides," she went on, "I have the endorsement of three of High Mountain's most opinionated ladies."

Nick cast a glance back toward the big house, distant over the ridge, where Vicky knew the trio was surely watching. Gossiping. She hoped not breaking out binoculars—she hoped that was beyond them. But these were the McNally sisters, after all. One could never be sure.

She turned to look at the house as well, only to realize how close it brought them to each other. She could smell whatever soap he'd used to clean up. She could feel him near, as if his skin gave off an electrical charge.

It should have been monumental. Huge and decisive. Instead, it felt like the easiest, most right thing in the world. Vicky closed the handful of inches between them and left a small, soft kiss on Nick's cheek.

She felt his whole body react. He startled, sucked in a breath, and looked at her with a wide-eyed wonder worthy of Taylor. For the longest moment, neither of them moved, frightened and fascinated at the same time. A breeze caught her hair and he moved to brush the lock off her forehead, his callused fingers grazing her cheek.

Vicky thought he was going to return the kiss. Surely, she'd tumble off the edge of the world if he did. So much was still thundering through her from the small kiss she'd given him. He certainly looked like he wanted to kiss her—really, truly kiss her, not a cautious peck on the cheek.

Instead, he cupped her face and tilted his head toward her until their foreheads touched. The tender gesture held more power than any kiss Vicky had ever known.

"I'm ready, too," he whispered right next to her ear.

Then, with one last searching of her eyes for her consent, Nick kissed her.

And she tumbled off the edge of the world. But oh, what a lovely way to fall.

Chapter Seventeen

"Mommy says it's Father's Day," Taylor announced when they were in the barn the next morning for another riding lesson.

Nick was painfully aware of the holiday and had no idea how to handle it. Vicky had said she was grateful to have this visit for Taylor, so Nick tried to make the day as perfect as possible.

"You're right, it is," he said as he hoisted Taylor up onto Dunk.

"Why aren't you somebody's daddy?" The question knocked Nick for such a loop that he was grateful he had the boy on the donkey already. He might have dropped anything he was holding at a question like that.

"How come you ask that?" he replied, just to give himself time to think up a better answer.

Taylor adjusted the riding helmet up a bit. "You look like one."

No one had ever said that to Nick before. And no one had ever told him he looked like a dad. And on Father's Day, to boot.

He busied himself cinching Dunk's saddle a bit tighter. "Really? What's a daddy look like?"

"Like mine. Mom shows me pictures."

That sent a blow to Nick's ribs. "Your dad and I don't look much alike." He added, "Our hair color is different, our eyes are different, and your dad was shorter than me." Having to use the word *was* when referring to Roger dug a jagged hole in Nick's gut. Taylor had been too young when Roger died to have any true memories of Roger. What do you do with that on Father's Day?

"Not that kind," Taylor said, as if it were obvious. Somehow Taylor's endless joy seemed to keep him from whatever sadness the day might bring.

"So what kind of different?"

"Mom says funny. And a big voice."

"Yeah, your dad was all those things. I really liked him." You'd think it would feel bad to talk about Roger like this on a day meant to honor fathers, but it felt easy. Important, maybe. Something that would mean a lot to Vicky.

"He's in heaven." Taylor said it so simply.

"I know." He wondered how much of Roger's death Taylor knew. He couldn't imagine giving the details of such a thing to someone so small. He himself was a full-on grown-up and those things still were a burden for him.

Nick gathered up the lead rope and began guiding Dunk and Taylor out of the barn into the big circle pen they now had all to themselves. Buddy, of course, came alongside. He hadn't let Buddy near at first, but it had become evident that while Buddy wasn't ready to be saddled, he was a perfect gentleman whenever Taylor rode his donkey friend. "I bet your dad wishes he were here to see you ride Dunk. I expect he can, now that I think about it."

"Mommy says he watches." After a moment or two, Taylor circled back to his original question. "So why aren't you anybody's daddy?"

"Haven't had the chance." The reply rang hollow in his chest.

"That's sad," Taylor pronounced. After another short pause, the boy added, "Mommy says you're nice."

Nick wasn't quite sure how to reply to that. "Does she now?" Some part of him wanted very much to hear more.

"So does Grannie."

Nick thought back to the setup the sisters had concocted last night. That was some meal. That was some kiss. He'd have to thank them today, if he could muster up the courage to face them without his face going red. No hope of hiding anywhere in this small town, was there?

"Mommy didn't before," Taylor said, somehow unaware of the secrets he was spilling. "First she was mad. " Taylor gave an impression of Vicky's fierce frown so adorable Nick could barely keep from laughing.

Hard to miss that. Vicky had practically spit nails the first time he showed up in the park and announced his presence and his desire to set things right between them. "You could see that, huh?"

"*Everybody* could see that," Taylor said with an eye roll that made him seem thirteen instead of three.

Nick couldn't resist. "And now?"

"She gets funny. Melty."

Taylor's version of what Nick suspected was a bit smitten—which is exactly how he felt himself—was alarmingly accurate. This was totally new territory for a man like himself. Weird, but welcome. And still fraught with risks—he shouldn't forget that.

"What do you think?" Was he asking Taylor his opinion of him? Of him with Vicky? All of it?

"I'm glad you came. You and Dunk and Buddy."

Nick could feel the grin spill across his face. "Me, too, Horsey Boy. Me, too."

The rest of Taylor's riding lesson flew by. Nick might never be able to explain the instant connections forged in this barn. Taylor and Dunk adored each other, the boy's affection drawing out trust and confidence in the donkey at an astounding speed. Young as he was, Taylor seemed born to ride. He had the instincts you couldn't really teach. Nick had no doubt Taylor would grow up to be a top-notch horseman if he chose. Maybe even on Buddy—and wouldn't that be a happy ending for this tale? And for a little guy with such a sad past, it warmed Nick's heart to see Taylor's grin of victory with every new skill.

Taylor warmed Nick's heart, period. *Adored* wasn't a word he ever had much use for in his life, but Nick adored Taylor. Wanted every good thing for the boy. Feasted on every inch of affection Taylor gave him—and Taylor gave his affection freely. The pint-size hugs that ended their riding lessons now were quickly becoming the best part of Nick's day.

Today was no different. After Taylor completed a circle of the round pen, holding Dunk's reins all on his own—with Nick close by and ready to intervene if necessary—Taylor's whoop probably echoed all the way back to the big house. Just because he could—and because it felt so good to do so—Nick gave a whoop right alongside him as he helped the boy off the donkey. Even Dunk gave a celebratory bray.

Nick had forgotten that sort of joy still happened in the world.

Just in case he needed an extra dose of reminding, Taylor's first response upon hitting the ground was to wrap his arms around Nick in a hug so fierce it brought him to his knees in front of the little guy. He found himself hugging Taylor back so tight it worried him that he might hurt the boy. Instead, Taylor squeaked and giggled. The sound lodged fluffy and bright in Nick's chest, like the prettiest of sunny summer clouds.

"Mommy likes you. A lot," he whispered in Nick's ear like the biggest of secrets. "I heard her ask Grannie if that was okay."

Given the setup of the picnic, Nick was pretty sure he knew Barb's answer. Still, it occurred to Nick he ought to ask his present companion's opinion. "That okay with you?"

"Sure," Taylor said without hesitation.

"Glad to hear it. I like your mom a lot, too. And I'd want you to be okay about that." He helped Taylor unbuckle the riding helmet, charmed at how it mussed Taylor's wavy brown hair. Roger's hair would go wild like that whenever he took off a work helmet, and Nick never missed an opportunity to rib him about it.

There were so many echoes of Roger in Taylor. At first it stung, tearing at the old wounds. Now Nick found the similarities settled on him like a peace. It had been a wild, impossible hope that Roger might have approved of what was growing between Vicky and himself. A hopeful wish he told himself when the doubts crept back up.

"Not Uncle Zack," Taylor said, pulling Nick's thoughts back to the present. "He doesn't like you."

Nick had not missed the dark looks Vicky's brother gave him whenever they happened to see each other in town. It wasn't surprising—nearly everyone had given him sideways glances when he first arrived. But the frost in Zack's regard had never thawed.

"Guess you can't please everyone, hmm?" Nick tried to keep his tone light and casual. Zack did not strike Nick as the kind of man to keep his opinions to himself, especially where his little sister was concerned.

* * *

I would have liked an easier Monday, Lord, Vicky thought as she closed the last file on her desk. Yesterday, Father's Day, had been hard. And today had been a long day. Edna Bogman had needed to say a permanent goodbye to her beloved collie, Butterscotch, this afternoon. Those appointments were never easy. Vicky shared Edna's tears, gave her a dozen hugs, and promised to help the woman find a new puppy when she was ready.

Veterinary care was clinical, but it was also about compassion. Vicky never belittled the deep grief a pet owner faced when saying goodbye to a treasured pet.

It didn't help that Zack walked through the front door with a sour look on his face.

Her brother needed a pet, Vicky thought, taking stock of her older brother's big, bold, successful life. He ran a prosperous ranch, but Vicky doubted any of the animals had reached the level of pet—meaning they were nothing more than just assets to Zack.

"Hello, Zack." She tried hard to inject some hospitality into her tone. "What brings you by?" She sat down on one of the waiting room vinyl couches, half out of weariness and half out of an attempt to soften whatever Zack had come to say.

True to his nature, Zack got straight to the point. "I'm worried about you."

In Vicky's experience, that usually translated to "I don't like what you're doing." It didn't take an advanced degree to guess that word of her and Nick had reached Zack. Most likely through Mom. She'd probably told him in the hopes of gaining his blessing. Clearly, the opposite had taken place.

"I'm fine, Zack. Rather well, actually." Might as well dive in. "What's got you worried?"

"Not what, who. I've been talking to Mom. About you. And him." The tone Zack gave the last word left little doubt of Zack's opinion.

Vicky thought to say, "Is that any of your business?" but swallowed back the retort. Zack was family. Zack had been very fond of Roger—in the small doses Zack was capable of. Vicky was grateful her brother remembered Taylor's birthday every year. In terms of stepping up to fill some of Roger's shoes in her son's life, however, it hadn't happened. Zack hadn't made any gesture to be around Taylor yesterday, and that hurt. Zack hadn't earned the right to pronounce judgment on her life.

"You shouldn't be trusting him. Come on—he shows up here with irresistible animals for Mom and the aunts? Worms his way into their lives and yours? All the while claiming to want to make good on something that can't be fixed. That doesn't strike you as suspicious?"

"I was suspicious. At first. And yes, Buddy and Dunk were brought here for that reason. That doesn't make their coming here wrong."

"It doesn't make it right, either. He's playing you, V. Using Taylor to get to you and ease his conscience. You've put Roger's death on him from the beginning. Now you just let it go, change your mind? Just because he tells you some very convenient tale that exonerates him?"

"The inquiry exonerated him, Zack. Remember?"

"You weren't so quick to agree with the inquiry before Nick showed up. I don't see how much has changed."

Vicky felt her guard shoot up. "I believed what I wanted to believe. It made it easier to get through those awful first months. I wanted someone to blame."

Zack threw his hands up. "Okay, so don't blame him. That doesn't mean you need to let the guy into your life like this."

Vicky pinned her brother with her fiercest glare. "Like what, Zack?"

Zack hesitated for a moment, as if debating whether or not to say whatever was on his mind. She knew her brother. It'd come out eventually. Might as well be now. "Like what, Zack?" she repeated.

"Like some kind of stand-in for Roger."

A moment of stunned silence stretched between them. Every doubt Vicky had tried to tamp down about the validity of her growing feelings for Nick roared to life. All the strength she'd managed to muster faltered at Zack's accusation.

Was what she felt for Nick real? Or just a lonely widow's ache to feel something—anything—in her world? Things had gone fast with Nick. A speed that felt out of control at times, no matter how careful they tried to be. A starving animal will eat just about anything you put in front of it—even something that could harm it. What about a starving heart?

The way Zack's words sliced through her made Vicky wonder how much painful truth was hidden in them. Most of her was sure Zack was wrong.

But not all of her. And so very much was at stake here.

She spoke slowly, carefully. "No one can replace Roger."

Zack matched her serious tone. "Does Nick know that?"

"Yes," Vicky replied. There was a sliver of uncertainty in her tone.

Zack put a hand on her shoulder. Vicky couldn't decide if it was compassion or condescension that fueled the gesture. "People are talking. That man is going to walk down the parade route with your son. With Roger's son. Are you sure that's what you want?"

Before Zack walked in the door, Vicky would have said yes, without hesitation. How had Zack roused so much doubt in her so quickly? Did that mean something? Did her brother see something she was hiding from herself because it felt so nice to feel something warm and hopeful again?

"Taylor wants it more than anything." That was true, but it felt like a cop-out of an answer.

Zack pounced on it. "Taylor is three. It's your job to protect him. What's he going to feel like when Nick heads back to the park service and you're right back where you started?"

They'd avoided talking about that. She and Nick were too happy to live in the bubble of Buddy, Dunk, and the farm. Kidding themselves that this would all turn out like some fairy tale. The question had lingered in the back of her mind—and surely must be doing so in Nick's—but they'd ignored it.

"I checked. Nick's medical leave only lasts so long. Then he goes back to whatever mountain they station him on next."

Vicky said, "Of course he goes back," just because she was too ashamed to admit she'd talked herself into ignoring that fact. That very important, life-altering fact. She ought to be annoyed that Zack had poked his nose into her life, but her brother had spoken the truth. This unlikely romance—and that is exactly what it had become—had an expiration date.

"He hasn't told you that, has he?"

It wasn't like that. It wasn't a manipulative omission. It was a hopeful disregard, if that made any sense. And so little about any of this made sense except for how good and right it felt. “We haven’t talked about it,” she answered.

“I know this has been hard. Roger’s death pulled the rug out from underneath you. Taylor was just a baby. It wasn’t fair. But that doesn’t mean this is the answer. Just please, consider the fact that you may not be seeing things clearly.” Zack shifted his weight. “Let me talk to him.”

If there was anything Vicky knew for certain at the moment, it was that Zack talking to Nick was not the answer. Nothing could come from the grilling Zack would surely give Nick. “I don’t want that.” Resentment bubbled up from inside her, and she let a bit of it show in her tone. “And as for someone filling the void left by Roger’s death, Nick has done a lot more in four weeks than you’ve done in three years.”

Zack turned and paced the room at the accusation. It was a low blow, she knew that. But it was also the truth. Had Mom come to her with this argument, Vicky would have listened more on account of how much Mom had invested in Taylor’s life since Roger’s passing. Master meddler that Mom was, she’d at least earned the right.

Zack had not. Zack was passing judgment by his own coldhearted standards. Something her brother excelled at.

“I tried,” Zack pronounced to the empty room. He started for the door. “I hope someone can get through to you before you do something foolish.”

Like what? Like fall for Nick Youngston? Let him into her heart and be grateful Taylor had done the same?

It was too late for that.

She didn’t say goodbye to Zack. She just threw the lock on the clinic door with a sharp click and choked back angry tears.

Chapter Eighteen

Nick was washing the mud off his truck in the driveway of the inn where he was staying when Vicky's truck pulled up.

Although she knew where he'd been staying, they'd never met here. Usually it was at the barn or at church service or the diner or some such place.

Or under that enormous tree he'd come to think of as theirs.

One look at her told him she'd been crying. It wrung his heart to see the red rims of her eyes, made him want to go after whoever or whatever had brought on those tears. Who dared to heap any more pain onto this extraordinary woman's life?

She walked up to him, planting her feet on the wet asphalt. "What happens when you leave High Mountain?"

It wasn't as if the question hadn't been haunting him for a while. "I don't want to leave."

He watched the words hit her, knowing it spoke of more than just some fixed date on a calendar.

Vicky swiped a hand through her hair. "Well, we don't always get what we want, do we?"

Nick pulled the tailgate down on his truck. He sat down and motioned for her to do the same. "What happened?"

"What are we doing, Nick? Are we just fooling ourselves that we can make this work? Wipe away all the history, what everyone thinks…"

Nick stopped her there, taking her hand. It was the first time he had taken her hand in public—not that the driveway of the Cedar Street Inn was especially public—but that didn't matter. Or maybe it was the perfect time for it to matter. "What did someone say to you?"

It wasn't hard to imagine. He'd caught the murmurs, the sideways glances, the way conversations died down if he walked by. Sure, the three sisters on the farm were warm and welcoming—it was like having a trio of grandmothers—but not everyone shared their generosity. Not everyone thought his appearance here was trustworthy.

"Zack just left the clinic. After hitting me with quite the lecture."

Nick had never spoken to Zack, but he didn't need to. The man's glare spoke loud and clear. Nick chose to ignore it, mostly because while Zack was Vicky's only brother, he didn't seem to be in Vicky's life too much. Nick took issue with that. Still, he paid more attention to the protective "don't hurt her" speech Grant Emerson had given him because he knew Meg and Grant and the girls were important people in Vicky's life. Grant's response came from care and support. Zack's likely came from judgment.

Still, a man can throw his weight around whether he's important or not. And Zack had clearly done just that. Even though Nick was sure the answer wouldn't be pleasant, he asked, "What did he say?"

"It doesn't matter."

He tightened his grasp on Vicky's hand. "It does. Because it obviously got to you."

She met his eyes. "He's wrong about you."

"That's nothing new to me."

"He's not wrong about us."

The way her voice caught snagged Nick's breath. "What do you mean?"

"What kind of future do we have?" she questioned. "You've got to go back to wherever the wildlife service stations you. And that could be anywhere in Montana. It could be clear on the other side of the state, and I can't leave High Mountain. Maybe this was never meant to be."

"Or maybe it was *exactly* what was meant to be. Not Roger's death—I don't for a minute think that was supposed to happen—but the healing. I think Cay's right. I think God sent me to Buddy and Dunk so I could bring them here. So I could be here. So we could work through all this."

She didn't respond. Strong as he knew Vicky to be, he could see the doubts still swirling in her eyes. There was a lot to doubt—mostly because all this still struck him as the most amazing, unbelievable twist of fate. Of God's surprises. What they felt now? The sure anchor she'd become in his life? The joy Taylor gave him? He didn't doubt those for a moment.

"If I think about it too much, I can come up with dozens of reasons why this shouldn't work."

"Oh, Zack gave me a list." Her shoulders sagged. "And I'd be lying if I said there wasn't a list pretty much like it in the back of my mind."

"Mine, too," Nick admitted. "But Vicky, I know what I feel. And I think I know what you feel. Don't you see? I came to settle things between us. To say my piece and maybe convince you not to hate me. And now? Now I care about so much more."

This was turning into some wild speech he had no right to be making, but Nick was determined not to let her slip from his life. He grabbed both her hands and held them tight. "I care about you. I believe in what we might have together. Right now it's more important to me than anything. I mean it when I say I don't want to go back. I want to stay here with you and Taylor and that ridiculous pair in the barn. I'll dig ditches or wash dishes in the diner before I go back to the wildlife office, because I want to be *here*. With you. Zack is wrong about me and wrong about us."

She held his gaze, and he watched some of the doubt fall away. "He's not alone."

"He could have a hundred people in High Mountain share his opinion and I still wouldn't let you go." The time had come to say it. "The thing I absolutely don't doubt here is that I've fallen in love with you. It's the last thing in the world I expected, but it's the thing I'm ready to fight for." He dropped her hands and placed his palms gently on either side of her face. Nick felt bold and brave when her eyes glowed at the contact. "I dare any of them to doubt the truth of what I feel for you. I love you." The declaration broke something open in his chest, and he repeated the words. "I love you. What else matters?"

Vicky closed her eyes for a long moment, and he watched a tear slip from her lashes and slide down her cheek. He wiped it away with his thumb, wishing he could wipe away every tear she'd ever had. She'd had far more tears than she should have had in her young life.

"I love you, too," she whispered back, and Nick felt the quiet words thunder through him. "It's all so impossible, but I do."

"I think God's in the impossible business. Seems like he shows up in bigger ways in places like this. You're God's gift to me, Vicky. You and Taylor both."

She kissed him. Right there on a truck tailgate in the inn

parking lot. This was how love heals. This was why love was the answer to everything.

She pulled back, and he realized she was crying again. Only these tears were different. He kissed them away, then kissed her forehead. *She means the world to me, Lord. Help me keep her.* Nick wanted to stand guard over her, protect her and Taylor from any threat, any of the town's wagging tongues. He wanted to walk down the town's main street not just holding Dunk's lead with Taylor in the saddle, but holding her hand. Suddenly the parade became about way more than raising money for a horse and a donkey.

It had become his—their—shout to the world.

Chapter Nineteen

Saturday morning, the day of the parade, proved to be a gloriously sunny day. Not too hot, a blue sky with just a touch of puffy clouds. It was perfect for a celebration.

Vicky fussed with the buckle on Taylor's overalls. "There," she announced, "You look great. Just like the sort of person who should be riding Dunk through town."

Taylor stuck his thumbs under the overall straps, grinned, and struck a pose straight out of a country and western song. "Where'd you learn that?" she asked with a laugh.

"Wally."

The week had proven what she'd already known: Taylor's confidence seemed to blossom with his riding sessions. Dunk brought something out in her son. Had it always been there, and she'd just been feeling too much grief to see it? Was he picking up on the return of joy in her life? Whatever the source, she was thankful. And today would surely add to the store of happy memories.

"Can we go yet?"

Taylor had been up with the sunrise, impatient to get what he called Parade Day started. He'd talked of nothing else all week. "All cowboys know you have to start an important day with a good breakfast," she replied.

Taylor wiggled into his blue muck boots—freshly cleaned up for the occasion—and plunked a cowboy hat onto his head. "Can I have French toast?"

She followed Taylor as he raced down the stairs toward the kitchen. "Sounds good to me. You can keep that hat on the other times, but you know you have to wear a riding helmet on Dunk."

"I know," he called over his shoulder. "Mr. Nick told me lots of times."

Vicky was being thankful Nick had focused on safety when a realization struck her. Taylor called Nick Mr. Nick, not The Horsey Man. What did that mean?

Taylor climbed up onto the counter stool while Vicky reached into the fridge for ingredients. "So now he's Mr. Nick, huh?" she ventured.

"Yep," Taylor offered without any other explanation.

They chatted about this and that while the French toast cooked. When she set the plate in front of him, he plopped a big lump of butter on the French toast and spread it around with the small, dull knife that came with his child's dishes and silverware. She always had to wait until just the right degree of "melty" had been achieved before Taylor allowed her to add the syrup. Some days she wondered if there was more syrup and butter on that plate than actual French toast.

Still focused on the spread of butter, Taylor said, "Mr. Nick gets all melty when he talks about you. Same way you do about him."

Vicky nearly dropped the syrup bottle. She was glad Taylor hadn't looked up, or he might have seen the shock on her face. "Melty?" She hoped her tone of voice came out something close to normal. It sure didn't feel like it.

"He asked me if it was okay that he liked you." Taylor seemed to have no sense of the weight of what he'd revealed.

"What did you say?"

"I said sure. You like him. I heard you tell Grannie."

Vicky planted one hand on her hip while she tried to casually pour syrup over the lake of butter on Taylor's toast. "You were supposed to be in bed when I had that conversation with Grannie." She had asked her mother what she thought about how strong her feelings for Nick were becoming. It didn't feel as if she could trust her own judgment. The whole situation seemed so impossible. Mom's assurance had been a welcome one.

"I got up for a drink of water. No big deal."

No big deal? The teenage words—and the fact that it seemed a very big deal to her—rendered Vicky speechless for a moment. Until she thought of another important question. "What do you think of Mr. Nick?"

"I like him lots. But not melty like."

Somehow, without even realizing it, Taylor had just given his blessing to her and Nick. It lit a hopeful glow in her heart that maybe, just maybe, they really could make this unlikeliest of romances work.

And it was a romance. She was in love with Nick Youngston. Was that enough to stand up against Zack and anyone else who couldn't see past the crazy circumstances of how they'd come together? How he'd returned to her life to heal it? This morning, catching Taylor's confident grin, it certainly felt like it. Vicky felt as if she'd finish this parade a whole new person. A whole new family, when she thought about it. How long had it been since the future unfolded itself with such hope before her?

"Well, mister, good thing we'll have at least one levelheaded non-melty person walking down that street with us."

Taylor scrunched his eyebrows at her as if to say *I have*

no idea what that means, then went back to devouring his French toast in record speed.

"Can we go *now*?" he asked, at least remembering to drag a napkin across his syrup-smeared chin.

Vicky grabbed her new straw hat that she'd purchased for the occasion. "I don't see how I can hold you off a moment longer, Horsey Boy."

Nick watched Vicky get out of her truck at the farm. In all his days he'd never seen a more beautiful woman. She had a glow about her this morning that went beyond excitement for the parade.

He probably glowed himself. He'd felt dumbstruck every moment since declaring his love for Vicky. And for Taylor. For all its impossibility, it was the most real thing in his life. The doubt, the disbelieving caution that had wrapped around his feelings for her, had fallen away as the week went by. In its place, a defiant, courageous hope had risen. One worthy of a parade. *Pretty spiffy timing there, Lord*, he mused as the glow in his heart doubled with Vicky's radiant smile.

Taylor raced toward him, beating Vicky by yards and wrapping his arms around Nick's legs. The press of those tiny arms was the second-best thing in the world. Vicky's embrace took top billing, as he hoped it would for the rest of his life.

Taylor craned his neck to look up at Nick. "It's parade day!"

"It is." He laughed, enjoying the boy's full-on joy.

"It took forever to get here," Taylor said.

"Just means we'll enjoy it more," Nick advised. He tipped his hat when Vicky came up. "Morning, ma'am."

She smiled at the surprising show of country gallantry. "Morning to you, too."

Nick enjoyed holding Vicky's glowing gaze for a moment before he felt Taylor tugging on his hand. "I wanna see Dunk. It's his big day."

He felt Vicky slip her hand easily into his on the other side. "Big day for everybody."

He wanted to kiss her right there and then. Nick was pretty sure that feeling wouldn't go away anytime soon today, if ever. Did the sun pour more brightly into the barn this morning, or was that just him?

"Hi, Dunk!" Taylor called.

Dunk's ears perked and the donkey trotted eagerly toward them. Buddy looked up from his morning oats, but didn't wander over. That wasn't unusual for Buddy—especially when someone interrupted his meal—but it made Nick wonder if Buddy didn't know what was coming. He'd been separating the pair for short periods all week in preparation for this big step.

"He's excited," Taylor said when Dunk produced an especially loud bray.

"Who wouldn't want to be heading a parade?" Vicky said. He caught a nervousness to her tone when she added, "Everybody will be watching."

It was true. Everyone would see them. Together. "Still good with that?"

A twinkle lit in her eyes. "A little *melty*, maybe, but good?"

Nick felt his eyebrows rise, flicking his glance down to look at Taylor then back up at Vicky.

"Somebody outed our mutual melty-ness at breakfast this morning," Vicky said, barely containing a laugh.

"Is that so?" To a three-year-old, that's probably exactly

what love looked like. Mutual melty-ness. The phrase would stick in his heart until his dying day.

"Can we put the saddle on now?" Taylor would have clearly started the parade in five minutes if given the chance.

"We got a while before we do that. And we've got to get him into the trailer, too. He can't walk all the way into town or he'll be too tired to do the parade." That wasn't exactly true—it was possible Dunk could make the whole trip—but Taylor would want to ride him the whole way and that wasn't a good idea.

Buddy still hadn't come over. "Besides," Nick went on, "we have to explain to Buddy that he's not coming." This was the one wrinkle in today's celebration. Nick was eighty percent confident Buddy would handle the separation well, but not one hundred percent. The short trial separations slowly got Buddy used to feeling safe in the barn and fields without his friend. And Buddy had done well. Whatever small risk they took leaving Buddy here without Dunk was a far better choice than taking the much larger risk of Buddy spooking in all the chaos of the pet parade. The simple truth was that while Dunk was ready for it—Nick would never allow Taylor to ride if he didn't believe that—Buddy was not.

The boy's lower lip stuck out. "Is Buddy sad?"

Nick tried to think of a way to explain it that Taylor would understand. "I don't think Buddy will like the parade as much as you will. He still likes it kinda quiet."

"Will he be lonely?"

Taylor's genuine empathy for the horse touched Nick. Taylor was so generous with his affections. *We could all learn a thing or two from him*, he thought as he ruffled the boy's hair. Roger had always talked about doing anything to protect his son, and Nick was coming to understand where that strong drive came from. This brand of selfless love was a new thing for him, but something he wanted in his life. Forever.

"He might be a bit lonely," Nick replied, choosing to be honest. "But it's only for a little while, and Buddy needs to learn to be on his own. This is a good next step." He'd been telling himself that all night when the tiny thread of worry would wind its way through his brain. Leaving Buddy home while Dunk walked in the parade was the wisest choice for everyone.

Nick's small worry died down when Buddy finally chose to walk over to where they were all standing. Nick stepped into the corral and walked up to the horse's side, running a hand down his back and speaking in steady tones. "G'morning there, Buddy. Big day for Dunk and Taylor here. We're gonna let you sit this one out at home, but we'll be back with some extra treats this afternoon."

"Promise," Taylor added.

Buddy chuffed, and Nick would have sworn the horse nodded in agreement.

He turned to Vicky, struck anew by the urge to pull her into his arms. *Get hold of yourself, man. You can't be distracted today.* Instead, he chose to wink at her, delighted at her surprised expression at the out-of-character gesture. Vicky was turning him into someone he didn't recognize. But someone he liked very much. All those songs about the love of a good woman must have it right.

"Okay, then. Time to get the tack loaded into the truck and the donkey loaded into the trailer," he announced. He turned to Taylor. "You can help with the tack, but the trailer's a tricky business. You need to steer clear and ride to the parade step-off in your mom's truck. Got it?"

"Got it," Taylor replied.

Together they piled the blankets, saddle, and other tack into Nick's truck bed. He hitched the secondhand horse trailer he'd helped the three sisters buy. He'd put up half the purchase price, another investment in Dunk's and Buddy's happy future here at the farm. If Dunk did well today, he might turn into a great spokes-donkey to promote the farm. The animal had charm, that's for sure—but it wasn't as if the sisters didn't have buckets of charm already between them. *I'm glad they like me as much as I like them.* No doubt, this place was starting to feel like home.

True to his donkey nature, Dunk wasn't exactly cooperative about getting in the trailer. Taylor looked a bit upset at Dunk's loud resistance, but Vicky explained that this was perfectly normal, and everything would be okay.

"C'mon, Dunk," Nick said as he came alongside the donkey for another pass at getting him up the ramp. "Make me look good for Taylor, okay?"

In the end, it took two more passes and a generous amount of carrots to get Dunk up the ramp and into the trailer, but the goal was achieved.

Taylor cheered. "On to the parade!" he proclaimed.

Nick gave himself the indulgence of a quick peck on Vicky's cheek as he rounded the trailer to get in the truck. Her cheeks pinked and her eyes sparkled. *You have fallen hard, Youngston*, he told himself even as he felt the smile on his face.

But, it wasn't hard. It was the easiest thing he'd ever done.

Chapter Twenty

I will remember this day for the rest of my life, Vicky thought as she watched Nick lift Taylor up onto Dunk's saddle at the parade step-off in town. Her son beamed. If he'd shown any fear on his first time riding Dunk, it was long gone. Dunk and Taylor were fast friends, and Taylor's confidence seemed to blossom with every ride.

Some other things were blossoming at the moment, too. Her love for Nick was nearly an overpowering thing today. His unexpected wink back in the barn sparkled in her chest. She felt her breath hitch for a moment when he slipped his hand in hers, sure the whole world was watching.

Some people did notice. Meg Emerson looked up from corralling Tabitha and Sadie, each of whom had one of the farm's dogs on a leash, and gave her a small, understanding nod. Each of the dogs the young girls walked wore wildly decorated collars—clearly the work of the girls. Grant raised an eyebrow in a silent "You're sure?" question. Vicky nodded to her cousin in reply.

Nick noticed the exchange and tightened his grip on Vicky's hand in reassurance. He leaned toward her and said quietly, "Gave me a talking-to, your cousin did. Told me if I ever hurt you I'd hear about it from him."

Vicky could only offer a chuckle. "That sounds like something Grant would say."

"I'd protect you and Taylor with my last breath," he declared. He said it quietly, simply, but Vicky knew he meant every word of it.

She saw Carly Peters next, pulling a wagon with baby Anson seated on board. Next to Anson was a brightly decorated hutch with two rabbits inside. Jack Peters walked next to her like the proud new father he was. Vicky was pleased to notice Anson's little wave was remarkably steady. That was good news for the little boy, who had come into the world with some challenges from spina bifida. An extraordinary surgery had given him the very best of chances, and the whole community rallied around the young family. So many of High Mountain's children knew Carly as the bunny lady, as she had worked with the farm to raise rabbits and helped the town's elementary school host rabbits as classroom pets. Would they show the same support to her and Nick? she wondered. Carly's and Jack's smiles as they noticed her hand in Nick's told her such a blessing was possible.

"Look at you, Taylor!" Pastor Jim called out as the parade made its way past the church. Her son waved back as if he were king of the world. Today, perhaps that's how he felt. *What a blessing it was.*

High Mountain loved its community celebrations, and today seemed no exception. People lined the street to watch a menagerie of animals go by.

"Will you look at all of them?" Nick remarked in amazement. Vicky wondered if Nick had ever been part of such a tight-knit community as High Mountain. He had always seemed a bit of a loner. She could have counted on the fingers of one hand the conversations they shared back when he was Roger's coworker. Field officers like he and Roger were loners by nature.

Watching Nick come out of that lonesome, sad shell was a wonder to see. Her profession gave her the privilege of watching healing all the time, but this healing was so very deep, so very personal.

"I think half my practice is out here," she replied, pleasantly amazed herself. "And a bunch of animals I've never seen." There were many dogs—some in creative outfits and others just walking along. One of Taylor's classmates from preschool walked with a bright red macaw offering a joyful squawk now and then. At least three sets of fish in ingeniously portable bowls joined the parade. And at least a dozen cats—which, knowing the nature of most cats, was rather amazing in itself.

Given the number of farms nearby, however, the term *pet* had a wide definition. There was a little girl dressed as Bo Peep—complete with shepherd's crook—leading the most adorable lamb. While Dunk may have claimed the spotlight, Vicky was certain that cute pair would get the most votes. Two speckled piglets trotted just behind, followed by a teenager pulling a wagon with a cage bearing the largest lizard Vicky had ever seen.

Nick kept a close hold on Dunk's lead rope, and Vicky could see him scan the scene and Dunk's ears to keep watch for any signs of trouble. "How you doing up there, Horsey Boy?" he asked as they made the second of three turns on the parade route.

"Great!" came Taylor's reply as he waved to yet another person in the crowd. Nick had not let go of her hand yet and sent an occasional squeeze of assurance as they walked. *It's okay to want this*, she thought to herself. *It's okay to have this. It's okay to be happy again.*

If anyone had asked her if Dunk's bray at that exact moment was a nod from both God and donkey, she would have said yes. After all, wasn't there some Sunday school story about the animals talking to announce the Christ child's birth? She of all people knew the healing power of animal companions. Wasn't today a celebration of just such an idea?

The parade ended with everyone gathered in the square at the center of town. As Vicky watched Nick help Taylor down from his mount, she remembered that this park was the very same place where Nick had first reentered her life. That had felt like an invasion. How quickly and fiercely her defenses had risen at the sight of him. So much pain and blame.

Now here she was with Nick, not against him. Everything felt lighter. She was thankful he'd come now. Thankful he'd made the tough choice to try and set things right between them. There was no conniving, no manipulation—Zack was wrong.

Still, that didn't stop Zack from coming up to her the moment Nick left to lead Dunk back into his trailer.

She leaned down to Taylor. "Isn't that Sammy over there on the swings? Why don't you go over there and play with him for a moment while I talk to Uncle Zack."

"Okay." Her son sped off in the direction of the swing set.

Zack stared over her shoulder in the direction of Nick and the trailer. "So you're with him now." How was it someone as hard-nosed as her brother had been raised by the same joyful parents as her mother and father?

"I don't expect you to understand," she replied. She refused to let him ruin such an amazing day.

"I don't. But if everyone didn't know, they know now.

You walked down the street like one happy little family, didn't you?"

Vicky lifted her chin. "Does that bother you? Would you rather I stay angry and unhappy? That Taylor be unhappy? I would think the way your nephew looked today should count for a lot."

Zack exhaled a breath. "Well, if this is what you want…"

It was a condescending sort of approval, but she'd take it. "Yes, as a matter of fact, it is. I won't say it's not complicated. I don't expect everyone to understand. But I do expect you to respect my choice and to show the same respect to Nick. If you can't do it for me, then do it for Taylor. I've never seen him happier." With a burst of courage, she added, "I'm happier. And I haven't been happy in a long time."

"If you're sure…" Zack replied.

"Of course I'm not sure. You can't ever be sure about such things. But I know what I feel, I know I trust Nick, and I know he cares a great deal about us." She stopped short of saying "loves," only because she knew it would irritate Zack, and she wasn't in the mood to get into it with him.

"I hope you're right." No one could infuse so few words with so much judgment like her brother.

"I hope for a lot of things I'd stopped hoping for. And that's a gift, Zack. I hope a gift like that comes to you someday soon, too." With that, Vicky found the grace to leave a small kiss on her brother's cheek and go push her son on the swings in the clear Montana sunshine.

Nick pulled the truck towing Dunk's trailer past the sign with the big red number three of Three Sisters Rescue Farm. "Welcome home, Dunk," he called through the truck's open back window, even though it was unlikely Dunk could hear him.

Nick didn't live here—Dunk did—but it was still amazing how he had come to think of the farm as home. The room at the inn was just the place he slept when he wasn't here.

He'd told Vicky and Taylor to lag a bit behind him. If there was any trouble with Buddy or with reuniting him with Dunk, Nick wanted Taylor far away. You could never forget that animals could be unpredictable. They could surprise you with the exact opposite of what was logical or what you expected. He hoped today wasn't one of those days.

The sisters were also still at the parade celebration, so Nick had the farm to himself. He rather liked the patch of solitude. So much had tumbled through his insides as he walked down the street with Dunk's lead in one hand and Vicky's hand tucked in his other palm. Connected to the things that mattered most to him now, the world had fallen into a wondrous balance. One he had never hoped to find. And, in all honesty, never thought he deserved to find.

Three Sisters Farm rescued more than just animals, but he expected those bighearted sisters knew that.

He caught a glimpse of his own smile as he checked his rearview mirror to pull the trailer up to the barn. Buddy was likely inside. He doubted the horse had ventured outside the safety of his stall without Dunk present.

Dunk gave a loud bray in greeting as Nick undid the latch on the back of the trailer. "Come on, boy. Out you go."

As if he was now an old hand at the ins and outs of trailer travel, Dunk came out easily. He gave another bray for good measure.

Something prickled down the back of Nick's neck when

no sound came from the barn in reply. Tamping down a sense of alarm, Nick kept his voice calm and steady as he pulled open the gate to the circular pen off the side of the barn. “Let’s go say hello to…”

No one. One look told Nick that the barn was empty. Buddy was gone.

Chapter Twenty-One

Buddy couldn't be gone. The day had been so perfect, such a celebration of everything Nick thought he could never have, that it simply wasn't possible. They couldn't have come so far—he, Vicky, Taylor, Dunk, and Buddy—only to meet with disaster now.

Not a disaster yet, Nick corrected himself, tamping down the fast-rising panic that threatened his common sense.

Still, there was no way to know how early in the day Buddy had escaped. No way to calculate how many hours he'd had to run or even wander. If something had spooked him—and that seemed the likely case—the impulse to run was the first thing rushing through a horse. With nearly the entire town having turned out for the parade, the chance someone had seen Buddy was slim. Nick didn't even know which direction to start looking.

He had to solve this. He had to fix this, and fast. He was too big to ride Dunk, and the farm had only a small tractor, not any kind of ATV that could keep up with a horse. Nick had to bank on the fact that Buddy hadn't run far or fast, that he hadn't been spooked but only gone off in search of his missing companion.

Step one was to secure Dunk. He could never hope to jump the fence as his larger friend had likely done, so that was a plus. Still, a quick look found that the corral's far gate was open. Had he somehow left it open in the process of getting Dunk into the trailer? That prospect made Nick sick to his stomach. He couldn't bear the idea that this huge loss was his fault.

On a quick impulse, Nick closed Dunk into a stall. Not only was it an extra level of protection, but Dunk didn't care for being confined to a stall and would likely make a lot of noise about it. That just might bring Buddy back if he was within hearing distance. It was a long shot of a chance, but Nick would take every advantage he could.

Step two was harder. Pulling out his phone, Nick clicked on Vicky's number and took in three deep breaths before she answered. "Don't come back to the farm yet," he stated the minute he heard the line connect.

"What? Why?"

"Buddy's gone." The words felt as if they punched him in the gut. "I'll find him—I promise you I will—but I don't want Taylor to know he's gone missing."

"How?" Despair filled her voice.

"Not sure yet, but the far gate was open when I got here, and Buddy was nowhere to be found."

"It's been hours." Nick could hear Vicky coming to the same worrisome conclusions he had. Buddy could be miles away by now. He could have even come to harm.

"I don't know anything yet. Just find some reason to keep Taylor away from here. I promise you I'll put this right. I just need time." There was no way Nick was going to let Taylor's amazing day end in disappointment. He would not suffer that kid shouldering one more loss in his life.

Vicky lowered her voice. "This isn't your fault, Nick."

Was that true? Nick had been the last person in the barn. He'd been focused on Taylor and Dunk. It was entirely possible—probable even—that this was his fault. The dark cloud of guilt, the one that had been his companion for so long and had finally lifted, sank back into place so fast Nick found it hard to breathe.

He didn't reply. He couldn't.

"Just keep him somewhere else," he finally said. "Anywhere else. I'll call you when I know more."

"That won't be easy." With a catch in her voice Vicky added, "He wants to be where you and Dunk are."

If she could have said anything that struck more deeply into his heart, Nick didn't know what it was. He said the only thing that seemed to matter at a time like this. "I love you. And him. I'll make this right."

Could he? All Nick knew was that he'd spend his last breath trying.

He clicked off the call and stood in the center of the corral, forcing his thoughts into some kind of order. Dunk began braying from behind him in the barn. He hoped he kept that up.

Nick scanned the landscape, trying to imagine Buddy's impulses. He wasn't any kind of skilled tracker for this sort of thing. But he knew animals and animal instincts. He walked to the gate. *Where would I go if I were Buddy?*

Even if the horse went through the gate, there was still the property fencing. There would likely be some physical clues where Buddy had jumped that fence. He hopped into the truck and began speeding along the fence line, looking for signs of Buddy's escape. *I could use a little help here, Lord*, he prayed. *Don't let this be how today ends.*

Back along the south end, Nick found what he was looking for. The barbed wire sagged in one place. When he got out to inspect it, he found a smear of blood. Thankfully, it looked like a small injury. Buddy had made it over the fence, but hadn't gotten caught too hard. Still, an injury could add to Buddy's stress level and keep him running farther.

Nick settled his nerves for what felt like the tenth time and tried to think. There was tree cover to his left, open fields to his right and ahead. Any of those directions might appeal to the horse. He needed to be in four places at once. He needed to be four people.

Or maybe he needed four friends.

He hadn't yet felt like the kind of person who could ask for favors in High Mountain, but there wasn't time to worry about that. He dialed Wally, Jack Peters, and Grant Emerson, quickly explaining the situation and asking if they'd find a way to leave the celebration without giving the situation away and join him on the farm to launch a search party.

Every one of them agreed instantly. Maybe he really had become part of the community. *I'd have preferred an easier way to find out, Lord.*

In the ten minutes it took the three men to drive through the ranch gate, Nick had shifted firmly into action. He had a map of the area spread out on his truck hood, marked with his best guess as the farthest perimeter and the likely places Buddy might be.

"We have got to find this horse," he declared to his makeshift team. In his heart he kept hearing *I have got to find this horse, I have got to make this right*, but Nick forced himself to use the word *we*. If he wanted to really be a part of his community, it was time to start acting like it.

"We will," Grant said. He was law enforcement. He knew how these things worked. He also knew that they didn't always end well, so Nick appreciated the promise in Grant's voice.

"I'll go here, it's the farthest distance," Jack offered. He had hitched a trailer with the ATV from his landscaping business and brought it to aid in the effort.

"I'll cover this end with the truck," Grant said.

"I'll take the tree cover on foot. He'll come to me, I hope, if he sees or hears me."

"That leaves this part for me," Wally said. "I got it covered." He gave Nick a steady glance. "We'll find him, Nick. We won't let Taylor down. Or you."

Mom came over across the grass of the park square, wiping her ice-cream-smeared hands on a paper towel. "Any word?"

Vicky felt her shoulders sag. "No."

"We've had a hot dog and some ice cream. And played two games. I'm running out of diversions."

Vicky was grateful for her mother's help, but it wouldn't change Taylor's insistence that they get back to the farm to see how Buddy and Dunk were doing. Pretty soon they were going to have to fess up to the situation back at the barn. Vicky's heart sank at the prospect of such a terrible ending to such a wonderful day. She knew Nick's heart was hurting just as much.

Mom stared after Taylor, who was thankfully occupied with Tabitha and Sadie over some lawn game set up on the other side of the square. "How'd Buddy get out?"

"The pen gate got open somehow, and Buddy went through. Nick texted that he found a spot in the far corner of the field where Buddy likely jumped the fence." Vicky hesitated before adding, "There was blood."

Mom pulled out her phone. "That can't be good. Time to fire up the prayer chain."

"For a horse?" Vicky asked, grateful, but wondering just

how far the legendary Grace Community Church prayer chain would go.

"Why not? God's creatures are God's creatures, no matter how many legs they stand on. If they prayed for the farm, why not for its residents?"

It made an odd sort of sense. And Vicky certainly wasn't ready to refuse any help to fix the way this day's victory was slipping out of her grasp.

"Done," Mom declared after tapping out a text message. Evidently the Grace Community Church prayer chain had gone digital. "How's Nick?"

"He blames himself. He thought he latched the gate, but things were hectic getting Dunk into the trailer." Vicky remembered the pain in Nick's voice. "He can't bear the thought of anything happening to Dunk or Buddy. He knows how much they mean to Taylor."

"It's pretty clear how much Taylor means to him," Mom said, grasping Vicky's hand. "How much *you* mean to him, too." She managed a wink. "That man's feelings were practically on parade today."

"I'm in love with him, Mom." It felt like an enormous admission. She scanned her mother's face for some sign as to how she viewed the news.

Mom's response was a warm smile. "I know, hon. After all, some things you can't hide from your mother. Or Taylor. I'm pretty sure he's figured it out." She chuckled. "Although 'melty' is a new one on me, that's for sure."

Vicky put her hand on her forehead. "How many people has Taylor told that I'm…melty?"

"Oh, I think it's just Cay, Peggy, and I, but you never can tell. And what your son didn't say, the look on Nick's face said loud and clear. That man's got 'I've fallen for her and I dare anyone to do anything about it' written all over his face." Mom tightened her grip on Vicky's hand. "Why are you worried about it? There's nothing but good in this, for you, Taylor, or for Nick."

"Tell that to Zack." If Nick could in any way be blamed for Buddy's disappearance, Vicky had no doubt Zack would cast the first stone.

Mom made a *pshaw* sound and waved her hands. "Zack has a lot to learn about how love and grace work." She paused for a moment before asking, "What is your heart telling you right at this moment?"

It was a powerful question. The day had been nothing short of glorious. She had felt transformed. Blessed as she watched Taylor's face and felt Nick's grasp. As if she'd finally found her way up out of the valley she'd been in for so long.

And yet, while disaster might be looming with Buddy's disappearance, that transformation hadn't gone away. She could face whatever the day might bring because she would be facing it with Nick beside her. Her mother was right—did it really matter what anyone else thought?

She smiled at her mother, not quite sure how to put all that into words. "My heart is telling me all I need to know."

Mom reached up to touch her cheek, a tender moment that seemed to reach back into years of love and assurance. "That's the whole point of love. No matter how today ends, you'll have that. Taylor, too." Her phone had started dinging with half a dozen texts and Vicky had no doubt it was the Grace Community Church prayer chain springing into action. Mom held up the phone. "And all these prayers."

Vicky looked out over the lawn to see Taylor coming toward her. "What do I tell him?" It was a silly question for someone who had helped dozens if not hundreds of families through a crisis with an animal they loved. She had a full store of professional advice for such moments. Still, this seemed so much more personal because of Taylor and Nick.

"The truth," Mom said. "That Nick will do everything he can to find Buddy. Jesus talked enough about lost sheep that I think he understands what one lost horse means to your family."

They'd become a new family, hadn't they? That was at the root of the extraordinary sense of safety, of security, she'd felt growing in her heart over the past weeks. A mother, her son, a horse, a donkey, and the most astounding man.

Buddy had to come home. Nick had to find him. But if the worst should happen, they still had each other. That was the truth that would carry Taylor through whatever happened next.

When her son came up to her impatiently whining, "Can we go to the barn *now*, Mommy?" Vicky knew what to say.

She hunched down to Taylor's height and made her voice as steady as she knew how. "We can, but you need to know something."

Much as she tried to hide it, Taylor picked up on her distress. "What?" he asked, alarm in his voice.

"Buddy got out of the pen while we were gone."

Escaped seemed like too drastic a word.

"Where is he?"

"Well," she replied, "we don't know yet. I think he was lonely without Dunk and went looking for him."

Taylor frowned. "We took Dunk away. That was wrong. He's sad."

She needed to try and put this in the right perspective for Taylor. "Keeping Buddy back in the barn was the right thing to do. He wasn't ready for a parade like Dunk. You and Dunk got to have your day, and there isn't anything wrong about that."

"But he's gone." With a quivering lower lip that struck deep in Vicky's heart, Taylor asked, "Is he gone forever?"

Those four words were like a knife to her chest. She gave Taylor the best assurance she had. "Nick is out looking for Buddy right now. And some of our friends are helping him. Even the grannies are praying that Buddy comes home soon."

A tear stole down Taylor's cheek. "He has to, Mom."

"I know. Dunk knows. You know. And I'm sure Buddy knows. So we have to be brave for a little while, okay?"

Taylor's nod was small and uncertain. "Okay." He took hold of her hand, and together they made their way to the truck.

As Taylor climbed into his booster seat, she texted Nick. Found him?

In reality, it was a fruitless question. Nick would have contacted her the minute Buddy had been found. Still, she couldn't help trying.

One lonesome word came back. No.

Followed by a more hopeful pair of words: Not yet.

Find him, she called to Nick in the silence of her mind as she pulled out onto the highway that led to Three Sisters Farm. *Bring him home, Nick.*

After all, Vicky was certain it was now Nick's home as well.

From the back seat of the truck cab she heard Taylor's small, wavering voice singing *"You Are My Sunshine..."*

She joined in, sure Nick was doing the same somewhere out in the field.

Chapter Twenty-Two

It felt as if hours had gone by.

Nick checked his watch to realize it had only been thirty minutes. Not that such a measurement mattered much if Buddy had been gone for hours. That horse could be anywhere. And who knew if he was in any kind of danger.

All the redemption he'd felt as his love for Vicky grew seemed to melt away. His soul sank back into the muck of guilt so fast it was getting hard to think clearly. One thought kept him focused, kept him going.

Taylor and Vicky.

Grant, Jack, and Wally had all come up short. Wherever Buddy had gotten to, no one had found him yet.

Yet. Nick clung to that word like an anchor in a storm.

Another twenty minutes went by without any sign of Buddy. Nick looked up to see the light starting to leave the sky. It was perfectly reasonable to believe Buddy could survive a night out in the open—it was summer and he'd regained all his strength.

But it was also reasonable to worry that any of the mountain's predators could do the horse harm. Especially if whatever wound the fence had given Buddy was leaving him lame or in pain.

Please, Lord, Nick prayed. *Grant me this. For them.* And

then, because he figured God knew it anyway, he added, *For me. I love them.*

He tried to ignore the ache of sorrow in his chest as he turned his steps toward the farm. It felt impossible to trust that everything would turn out okay. Still, he knew with a certainty that overpowered everything else, that he'd stay and see Vicky and Taylor through however this turned out.

High Mountain was his home now.

He just had to trust that it had become Buddy's, too.

There.

Just beyond the next crop of trees, Nick spotted the patch of cream and brown. He dashed closer to get a better look while his heart skipped a handful of beats.

Another movement brought the horse's head into view and told him all he needed to know. He whistled to the horse the way he always had and began running as quickly as he dared in Buddy's direction.

Thank You, God.

He approached Buddy slowly, talking in low and steady tones. "Hey there, big guy. You had us all worried." He put his hand on Buddy's neck and gently clipped a lead onto Buddy's halter. Once secured, Nick lay his head against the horse's neck, filled with relief. Nick could have sworn he felt the same relief in the horse, saw the gratefulness to be found in Buddy's large brown eyes. "I'm sorry we took Dunk away from you, but don't pull a stunt like that again, okay?" he whispered. "Too many people need you back at the farm." He thought of Taylor and Vicky, and his heart finally let go of the fear and tension that had wrapped around his chest since the moment he stepped into the empty barn.

Nick glanced down at the wound on Buddy's fetlock, glad to see it was small. "Can you walk home? It'll take a while to send for the trailer, and everybody's waiting."

He led Buddy toward the farm. Surely Vicky could tend to whatever Buddy needed when he got back to the barn. The most important thing was to get Buddy back home.

Nick gave a tug on the lead and took off in the direction of the farm as fast as Buddy could manage.

But not before he sent a four-word text to Vicky, Jack, Wally, Grant, and Cay.

Found him. Coming home.

"Where is he, Mommy?" Taylor kept asking over and over, slowly losing his battle with tears each time he asked.

"We'll find him, honey," she assured her son, only it was starting to feel like a thin hope. Vicky couldn't bear the idea of another loss for his young life. Buddy and Dunk had come to mean so much to him. After the amazingly happy ending of Nick's arrival in High Mountain, it just didn't seem possible that Buddy could be gone forever. She clung to hope, but it was getting harder.

Just when she thought she'd have to drag Taylor home to bed in what surely would be a bout of tears, her phone dinged an incoming text.

Found him. Coming home.

Vicky rushed to Taylor and showed him the text even though he couldn't read. "Nick found him! Buddy's coming home!"

Taylor's face broke into a wide smile. "Hooray for the Horsey Man!"

She hugged her son. "Hooray for the Horsey Man indeed."

Grant, Wally, and Jack made it back to the farm before Nick, given how Nick and Buddy were on foot. When Nick and Buddy finally came up over the ridge into view, a cheer went up all over the farm. Even Meg and her daughters had come over from their home, as well as Cay, Mom, and Peggy.

Nick was certainly getting a hero's welcome. Vicky was deeply grateful, her heart bursting at the sight of him. What a change from the day six weeks ago when she'd bristled at him at the park.

It touched her deeply that while Nick held her eyes for a long moment, he went first to Taylor. A broad laugh escaped him as Taylor flung himself at Nick, wrapping his small arms around Nick's broad chest and burrowing his head against Nick's neck. Her love for him seemed to double at the sight.

She let them have that precious moment, busying herself with inspecting the wound on Buddy's leg. It was minor—not much more than a scraping from barbed wire as the horse evidently jumped the fence. A quick application of an antibiotic and a bandage made short work of the equine first aid. Dunk stayed right beside Buddy the whole time, watching over his friend as if to say, "I'm sorry I left you." In her imagination, she envisioned Dunk telling Buddy all kinds of grand tales of his time in the spotlight.

Filled with relief, Taylor began yawning almost instantly, and Vicky knew she'd need to get her son home soon. Still, she desperately needed a few moments alone with Nick. "Go say good night to Grannie, okay?" she asked.

The moment Taylor trotted off in the direction of the big house porch, she felt Nick's hand pull her into the shadow of the barn wall. He drew her close and kissed her with such boundless emotion she thought she'd never catch her breath again. Everything they'd come through, all the distance they crossed to reach each other, seemed wrapped up in the embrace they shared. Vicky clung to him as fiercely as Taylor had, awed by the love filling all the places fear had been.

"Thank you," she managed to whisper, almost amused at how breathless she sounded. "I'm so glad you're here."

"I feel like I've waited a lifetime to hear you say that," he said softly, emotion catching in his own voice.

Vicky looked into his eyes. His gaze was tired and relieved and full of love. "Don't ever leave."

"I don't plan to. Ever. After all, seems I've got a family of five now."

"Five?" she teased, even though she had an idea what he meant.

"You, Taylor, and those two troublemakers back there." He cocked his head in the direction of the barn, still spilling light out onto the grass beyond them.

"We all need you."

Nick ran his hand through a lock of her hair. "You got it backward. It's me who needs you."

"That's just it," she corrected, "We need each other. As my mom says, that's how love works. Mutual melty-ness and everything."

He laughed. "Mutual melty-ness, huh? Who made that up? Taylor?" Even his smile had changed in his time in High Mountain. The grin came easily and reached all the way to sparkle in his eyes.

"Me, just now."

"Love works in mutual melty-ness. Guess I'm just figuring that out."

"We all are." She leaned close. "Welcome home, Nick."

His answer was another breathtaking kiss that made Vicky melt all over again.

Epilogue

Nick had never been to a barn dance.

Still, it was just what he expected: a dance held in the Three Sisters Rescue Farm barn. Buddy and Dunk and the dogs had been moved to one of the outdoor pens, and the place had been strung up with party lights, set up with tables that were groaning under piles of good food, fresh hay bales covered in colorful tablecloths for sitting, and a ridiculous number of streamers. It was hard to imagine a happier place anywhere on earth.

The September evening air still held the warmth of summer, but hinted at the spectacular colors of fall that would fill the mountains in the coming months.

No one had ever given a specific reason for the party. Evidently, the three sisters considered no reason necessary. "It's simply because parties are fun," Vicky had said.

High Mountain was teaching Nick a lot about life and happiness and joy. And he'd become an eager student. Vicky didn't know that Nick had gone to the sisters with a reason of his own to add to the party. Delightful coconspirators that they were, Barb, Cay, and Peggy had agreed to his plan in an instant.

Just after dinner, Nick tugged on Vicky's hand. "Let's go sit on the porch for a minute."

They wandered out of the barn's light, stepping across the stretch of grass between the barn and the big house's wide front porch. Heart pounding, he settled them in on the big porch swing.

"Look at it all," Vicky said, contentment in her voice.

"Beautiful," he agreed. The whole scene looked like something out of a movie. It was the perfect place to ask an important question, but nerves still jangled every inch of his skin. He took in every detail of the woman next to him—the curve of her jaw, the way her lashes framed her eyes, the dimple that appeared on one cheek when she smiled. She smiled so much more now. The same could be said of himself. Life here had become something he'd never thought he'd ever deserve.

A yawn rose up from his chest, and he tried with annoyance to stifle it.

"Tired?" she asked.

He'd put in long days at his new job managing the school fields and grounds. School would be starting soon, and there was a lot of work to be done. "Only a bit," he replied, putting his arm around Vicky and pulling her close.

He was tired, but he thought he'd downed enough coffee not to be tired for this. Anxiety had strung his nerves tight all evening.

Vicky lay her head on his shoulder, and then everything seemed downright perfect. He shifted toward her—enough to look in her eyes but not enough to pull her out of his embrace. "I've got something for you."

He'd been doing that a lot lately. Bringing her little things. A small bouquet of flowers, coffee from the diner, those cookies she liked from the bakery on the corner. He enjoyed indulging her, indulging this new generous spirit she woke up in him.

This was not a little something. This was a great big something. "I asked Taylor if it was okay to give this to you. He said yes."

Nick pulled the small blue velvet box from his pocket. "You've changed my life, Vicky Siden. You and Taylor. I'll never stop being grateful for all this. I'll never stop loving you. So I figured it was time we made it permanent." He opened the box to reveal a ring that sparkled in the porch light. "Will you spend the rest of your life with me? Will you marry me?"

Her reply was marvelously instant—he barely got the question out before she said "Yes!" and pulled him closer. "Yes," she repeated as he slid the ring onto her finger. "I want to spend the rest of my life with you." Then, as she realized what he'd said earlier, she looked up at him. "You asked Taylor if it was okay?"

He grinned, no longer the least bit tired. "Figured I ought to. He approves, by the way. Although he thought I ought to ask Dunk and Buddy for their opinion, too."

Vicky laughed. "Did you?"

"No," he admitted. "They may be family, but you two were the only votes I cared about."

"Family," Vicky echoed with a sigh. "I like the sound of that. I love our family. And I love you." She kissed him, and he kissed her right back.

Until they heard a cheer rise up from the barn.

"How did they…?" Nick asked, feeling too much on display. This was supposed to be a private moment.

Vicky was laughing. "I was wondering why Mom insisted on bringing binoculars to the party."

Nick could only surrender to the absurdity of the moment. “Will it always be like this?”

Vicky smiled and kissed him again, waving to the still-cheering spectators in the barn. “I sure hope so.”

* * * * *

Dear Reader,

A true friend is a great blessing—in both the human and the animal world. True love and the power of the truth can transform lives. And we all know God is in the transformation business.

All of us travel the path to healing at some point in our lives. It can be long and twisting, steep and demanding, or straightforward. Still, healing always asks a lot of our hearts and minds. Nick and Vicky have a long distance to travel to the healing each of them needs. It's a good thing they have Buddy and Dunk—and even young Taylor—to show them the way. I hope their story gives you encouragement for whatever healing journey you may be traveling.

My thanks to Shayna Mann and the fine folks (hoofed and otherwise!) at Agape Acres farm, who helped me learn the details of what the three sisters would face with Buddy and Dunk. You can learn more about them and their mission at www.agapeacrescarolinas.com/

Thank you so much for this return visit to High Mountain and Three Sisters Rescue Farm.

I am always delighted to hear from readers! You can reach me at allie@alliepleiter.com as well as Instagram (@alliepleiterauthor), Facebook (@alliepleiter), and my website alliepleiter.com.

Blessings,
Allie